W9-DEH-635

**"Come with me to the party, Elizabeth,"
Culley said.**

"I don't have anything to wear," she murmured.

"Wear anything. You'll look beautiful no matter what . . ."

Culley just sort of ran out of words; Elizabeth's fingers were tracing exquisite patterns over his collarbone. Gazing into her eyes made him feel as if he were standing on a cliff high above the ocean—he could easily succumb to vertigo if he looked too long. "Elizabeth . . ."

He released her wrists, but somehow, rather than severing the contact between them, it was as if he'd released a brake. Her hands slid upward to his shoulders, then his neck. His hands moved along her arms, pushing the sleeves of her sweatshirt out of the way, stroking her soft skin.

He lowered his head and felt her small hands, those delicate fingers, weave through his hair. He closed his eyes and felt the sweet stirring of her breath on his lips. He growled something—it might have been an oath or a prayer, or even her name—and, cradling her head in his hands, slid his fingers into the flame-gold masses of her hair, claiming her mouth with his. . . .

WHAT ARE *LOVESWEPT* ROMANCES?

They are stories of true romance and touching emotion. We believe those two very important ingredients are constants in our highly sensual and very believable stories in the *LOVESWEPT* line. Our goal is to give you, the reader, stories of consistently high quality that may sometimes make you laugh, sometimes make you cry, but are always fresh and creative and contain many delightful surprises within their pages.

Most romance fans read an enormous number of books. Those they truly love, they keep. Others may be traded with friends and soon forgotten. We hope that each *LOVESWEPT* romance will be a treasure—a "keeper." We will always try to publish

*LOVE STORIES YOU'LL NEVER FORGET
BY AUTHORS YOU'LL ALWAYS REMEMBER*

The Editors

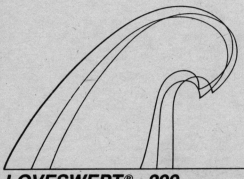

LOVESWEPT® • 299

Kathleen Creighton
The Sorcerer's
Keeper

 BANTAM BOOKS
TORONTO • NEW YORK • LONDON • SYDNEY • AUCKLAND

For Wendy, and for her beautiful mommy,
Dawn, who first introduced me to the "terror's"
of parenthood.

THE SORCERER'S KEEPER
A Bantam Book / December 1988

LOVESWEPT® and the wave device are registered
trademarks of Bantam Books, a division of
Bantam Doubleday Dell Publishing Group, Inc.
Registered in U.S. Patent
and Trademark Office and elsewhere.

All rights reserved.
Copyright © 1988 by Kathleen Creighton.
Cover art copyright © 1988 by Penalva.
No part of this book may be reproduced or transmitted
in any form or by any means, electronic or mechanical,
including photocopying, recording, or by any information
storage and retrieval system, without permission in
writing from the publisher.
For information address: Bantam Books.

If you would be interested in receiving protective vinyl
covers for your Loveswept books, please write to this address
for information:

Loveswept
Bantam Books
P.O. Box 985
Hicksville, NY 11802

ISBN 0-553-21950-2

Published simultaneously in the United States and Canada

Bantam Books are published by Bantam Books, a division
of Bantam Doubleday Dell Publishing Group, Inc. Its trademark, consisting of the words "Bantam Books" and the
portrayal of a rooster, is Registered in U.S. Patent and
Trademark Office and in other countries. Marca Registrada.
Bantam Books, 666 Fifth Avenue, New York, New York 10103.

PRINTED IN THE UNITED STATES OF AMERICA

O   0 9 8 7 6 5 4 3 2 1

One

"I'm not goin' in there," the pirate said, shaking his head. "*You* go."

The vampire took a step backward. "Not me."

"Chicken," said a boy wearing the gold mask and helmet of Solar the Antarian. A keen October wind gave his iridescent cape a swirl, a rather nice, heroic effect that was entirely wasted on his two companions.

The pirate scraped at the sidewalk with his shoe. "I'm not chicken," he said reasonably. "The gate's shut. That means they don't want any trick-or-treaters."

"All the lights are on," Solar the Antarian countered. "My mom says if they don't want kids to come, they turn the lights off and pretend nobody's home. I say we ought to go up to the door."

"Sure is a spooky old place." The vampire was peering through the wrought iron bars of the gate. The others moved up beside him. There was silence while they watched dry leaves scuttle down the long, curving driveway.

"My mom says a scientist lives there," Solar the Antarian said.

"Yeah, a *mad* scientist, I bet," the pirate muttered.

"Hey, yeah—Frankenstein!" Getting into the spirit

of the thing, the vampire raised his shoulders up to his ears, dangled his arms, rolled his eyes up, and began to walk stiff-legged in circles.

"Maybe he's a witch!"

"Witches are girls, stupid!"

"Okay, a wizard, then."

"A sorcerer! Like the one in Mickey Mouse!"

Upon hearing this, the "sorcerer" found it difficult to smother his laughter. He was also having a hard time staying on his perch, which was about six feet above the three boys' heads, on the limb of a large magnolia tree. His task was further complicated by the fact that he held a very disgruntled tomcat in his arms.

As his burden began to struggle in earnest, he whispered, "Shh . . . easy does it. Hold on a minute—" And then, "Ow!" That was followed by some *sotto voce* cursing.

The cat's side of the conversation lent a great deal to the atmosphere of the evening.

"Well, Albert, I hope you're satisfied," Dr. G. Cullen Ward, Cal Tech professor, nuclear physicist of some repute, and potential Nobel prizewinner, said to the cat a moment later as he watched the three boys hightail it down the street.

He really was sorry to see them go. He didn't get many trick-or-treaters, even when he remembered to leave the gate open, and it looked as if the basket of candy bars his mother had left on the table in the front hall was going to be around to test his will-power for quite a while.

With a sigh, he tucked the cat under his arm and began the process of extricating himself from the tree. The cat, whose full name was Albert Einstein, let him know in no uncertain terms that he considered that sort of cavalier treatment far beneath his dignity.

"It's your own fault, you know," the physicist said without rancor as he nursed a scratch on his thumb.

"Next time I think I'll let you take your chances. Any black cat dumb enough to go out carousing on Halloween night deserves what he gets."

He pulled the gate open and fastened it back, in the vain hope of encouraging late trick-or-treaters to enter. As he walked to the house, absently stroking the cat's head, he tried to see his home as the three routed revelers might have seen it. He was sorry the neighborhood children found the place so intimidating; he'd always been fond of it, himself. He'd grown up in the house, lived there all his life, in fact, except for the years he'd spent away at college. He'd brought his bride to this house.

And it had been a happy house, full of warmth and laughter. He'd been an only child, but he'd never lacked playmates. The walls around the estate had given the neighborhood kids, not to mention their mothers, a sense of security, while the woodsy, unmanicured grounds had afforded them freedom to explore and pretend to the limits of their imaginations.

A happy place. As he often did when deep in thought, he forgot whatever else he was doing. He stopped walking, forgot to stroke the cat. When had that changed? When had his home become the neighborhood haunted house?

Leaves tumbled over themselves along the path ahead of him as if anxious to be out of his way.

He noticed that while he'd been pondering, dusk had become night. The moon had risen behind the house, not a full moon, but close enough. As a child, he remembered, he'd spent a lot of time wondering about the moon, what it was made of, and what it would take to go there. He'd always expected to go there, and was still vaguely disappointed that, while his mind had frequently gone where no man had gone before, his feet had remained firmly earthbound. He spent his time these days wondering about such things as subatomic particles, quarks, isotopes, and beta decay. The moon held no romance for him now.

But he had to admit there was a certain chilly beauty about the moonlight tonight, the way it threw the turrets and cupolas of his house into Gothic silhouette. It looked . . . he searched for and finally found the word: Lonely.

Shifting the now placidly purring cat in his arms, Culley, as he preferred to be called, walked on. No doubt about it, the old homestead could do with a few kids running around, wading in the lily pond, chasing squirrels through the woods, building tree-houses. And that was too bad. Because he was a long way from being ready to start thinking about marrying again, much less having kids.

No, Culley told himself, maybe the place looked lonely and haunted, but it suited him just fine. The solitude was what he needed, both for healing . . . and for other things.

And tonight it was long past time for him to get to those other things. As he went up the flagstone walk, the lighted attic window, the one high up in the steeply gabled roof, stared down at him like an accusing eye, reminding him that he'd left poor Princess Kerissa in the clutches of the dreaded Tularian Bat People!

So it was that Culley's mind was once more off in an alien world when he passed through his front hallway, which was why he didn't even glance at the basket of candy bars on the table there, or notice the small white rectangle propped against it. Halloween and trick-or-treaters, as well as virtually everything else of this world, had been left light years behind.

He was vaguely aware of a niggling notion that he was forgetting something, but he got that feeling often, and had learned to ignore it.

He'd taken about two steps up the wide, curving staircase when Albert suddenly sank his teeth into his forearm, bringing him rudely back to earth and reminding him of both the cat's presence and of his need to be fed. Thankful at least to know what it was he'd forgotten, Culley muttered, "Oops, sorry, old boy!" Then, backtracking, he detoured to the kitchen.

He located a can of cat food and a can opener without too much difficulty, and put one to work on the other while Albert watched with heavy-lidded disdain. "Hah!" Culley announced in triumph as the lid popped off in fine form. Albert sighed and looked away.

"Okay, where's the missus?" A scratching noise from the door to the back porch answered Culley's question. With a muttered "Damn!" he went to unlatch the kitty door—something else he'd forgotten. The feeling began to nag at him again, but he told himself if it was anything important, his mother would have left him a note.

A small, cream-colored cat with distant Siamese antecedents shot through the kitty door looking frantic. While Culley was finding a fork and using it to divide the can of cat food between the two bowls on the floor, she wrapped herself around his ankles and complained loudly about her ill-treatment.

"Yeah, Prissy, you're getting too fat anyway," Culley muttered when the nagging had been replaced with wet, sticky eating noises. Bending down to give the cat a perfunctory scratch behind the ears, he said, "Better watch it. Albert likes his ladies on the svelte side."

As he tucked the fork in his shirt pocket and put the empty cat food can in the refrigerator, his mind was already off again, voyaging in alien waters. He gave no further thought to what it was he might have forgotten.

Elizabeth Resnick peered at the brass numbers on the massive stone gatepost, illuminated clearly by her high beam headlights. Nope, no mistake.

"Why stoppin', Mom?" Wendy, her two-and-a-half-year-old daughter, had begun to rock impatiently in her car seat. "What you doin'?"

"Having second thoughts," Elizabeth muttered.

"What?"

"Nothing, sweetie. Sit still, okay?" She took a deep breath, put her ancient Toyota in gear and crept through the gate. It was open, at least, so Dr. Ward must be expecting her. She only wished *she* knew what to expect. Grace Ward had been disquietingly vague about her son, except to say that final approval, of course, would have to be up to him.

"Gramma's house?" Wendy ventured, sounding doubtful.

"No, baby," Elizabeth told her gently, "this isn't Gramma's house." As always, she fought to keep any negative inflections out of her voice when she spoke of the Resnicks; the last thing she wanted to do was let her own fears contaminate Wendy's love for her grandparents.

The driveway's gentle curve carried them through trees and shrubbery made spooky by moonlight and suggestion. *All Hallows' Eve . . .* To keep from being intimidated by the grounds around the house, Elizabeth tried to imagine them in daylight with birds singing in the trees and squirrels rummaging busily among the fallen leaves. In the spring, she told herself, there would be crocuses and daffodils. This would be a lovely place for a child to play.

In front of the house the gravel drive made a sweeping circle around a large lily pond with a stone fountain in its center. Elizabeth pulled the car to a stop between it and the front steps, turned off the motor and lights, and sat for a moment, just staring up at the big house.

"Trick 'r treat?" Wendy asked hopefully.

"No." Elizabeth reached for the door handle. "No more trick or treat. I told you, remember? Mommy has to talk to a man about a job."

"Talk to a man?"

"Right."

"Man's house," Wendy announced, pointing over her mother's shoulder as Elizabeth bent to unbuckle the harness of the car seat. "Big house."

"It certainly is," Elizabeth agreed, mentally squaring her shoulders. After all, while *big* meant lots of work, it also meant lots of room. Room for her, and for one very energetic little girl.

Taking a measure of courage from the small hand which had crept into hers, Elizabeth marched up the flagstone walk and pressed the doorbell. For good measure, Wendy pressed it, too. Twin foghorns echoed and resounded beyond the massive wooden door, delighting Wendy, who gave a little gasp and turned a pixie smile upward. The sight of her daughter's sparkling eyes and open face, still framed by the red hood of her Halloween costume, gave Elizabeth a squeezing sensation in the vicinity of her heart.

"Someone's comin'," Wendy said in a breathless whisper.

"You think so?" Elizabeth murmured doubtfully, reaching for the iron knocker. Just as she grasped it, the door opened abruptly inward, yanking her forward over the sill. There was an awkward moment while she struggled for balance, and strong hands reached reflexively to steady her. And then there was silence.

It was the kind of silence that follows lightning— tense, waiting for the clap of thunder. As she stared openmouthed at the man before her, Elizabeth even found herself silently counting, one . . . two . . . three. . . . But except for that, her mind was a blank.

"Trick 'r treat?"

As thunderclaps go, it wasn't much, but it did the trick. The world began to turn again. Elizabeth's mind began to function; she drew breath, felt her heart beating, became aware of an unaccustomed warmth in her cheeks and on her arms where a pair of masculine hands were touching her.

She realized that the man to whom the hands belonged was only a head taller than she was, no more than average height, and that he was surprisingly young. He didn't look much like her idea of a nuclear physicist, but he wasn't in any way intimidating. There was no reason why she should have a sudden attack of butterflies in the stomach, or a wildly pounding heart. Perhaps, she told herself, her nervousness had something to do with the fact that his dark brown hair looked as if he'd just gotten out of bed; or the fact that, behind a pair of dark-rimmed glasses, his brown eyes had focused on her with warm but intent and puzzled stare.

Something about that stare made her feel off balance, uncertain. Fighting to regain the composure she'd somehow lost, she shook her head and said, "Wendy, no—" just as the man ventured, "Trick or treat?"

"No, that isn't—"

The bewildered look left the man's eyes; they widened in a look of incredulity and delight that made him seem almost boyish.

"Trick or—hey, that's great! I didn't think anybody . . . Wait a minute now, I know there's something here somewhere. . . ." He looked around. With a triumphant "Ah!" he snatched up a basket of candy bars, knocking over a white envelope in the process. Without looking at the envelope, he picked it up and stuffed it into his shirt pocket.

That was when Elizabeth noticed the fork. The man had a fork in his shirt pocket. Not a clean one, either; bits of something resembling meat loaf were clinging to the tines.

Of course. A smile blossomed inside her, banishing butterflies. What was it Grace Ward had said to her? "My son needs a keeper." Not housekeeper. Just a keeper.

While Elizabeth was still gazing in awe at the fork, Dr. Ward dropped to one knee in front of Wendy.

"Well now, let's see. Are you Little Red Riding Hood?"

Wendy's head bobbed in vigorous confirmation. "Riding Hood!"

Too bemused, for the moment, to intercede, Elizabeth stared down at the man she'd come to ask for a job. She observed that his hair was in need of a trim. She noticed the way the muscles in his back and shoulders changed shape beneath the fabric of his shirt when he reached to touch her daughter's cape.

Planting her tongue in her cheek, Wendy took a tentative step forward and touched the man's face with a chubby forefinger. And somewhere deep in her midsection, Elizabeth felt that warm, squeezing sensation again.

Wendy turned wide blue eyes on her mother and stated with absolute conviction, "That's a man."

Yes, it certainly was. And to her profound dismay, Elizabeth was beginning to realize that he was a very attractive one, too, something his mother had neglected to mention.

"Daddy?"

"Oh boy." Laughing apologetically, Elizabeth drew her daughter close against her legs. The man stood up, looking understandably taken aback. Elizabeth held out her hand. "I'm sorry, she's at that age. Dr. Ward, I'm Elizabeth Resnick."

The warm, yet puzzled frown was back again. The hand that closed around hers was reassuring, but reserved. "Elizabeth?"

"Elizabeth Resnick. Your mother sent me. It's about the housekeeper's job. She said you'd be expecting me." What Grace had actually said to her, Elizabeth remembered, was, "I'll tell him you're coming, but he will undoubtedly forget. I'm afraid you are apt to be on your own."

Culley closed his eyes for a moment and let go of an exasperated breath. "So that was it," he said under his breath. "I knew there was something . . . Grace—my mother—did mention you. But she usually leaves me a note. I don't know—"

"Perhaps," Elizabeth suggested gently, "that's it in your pocket."

"Ah." He smiled apologetically, patted his pocket, then carefully removed its contents. After glancing at the fork without much surprise, he laid it aside on the table and opened the envelope. A moment later he dropped his mother's note on top of the fork and dragged a hand through his hair, a gesture which certainly explained its state of disarray.

"Look, uh, Elizabeth, I don't know about this housekeeper business. It's a big house, but with just the two of us living here, there really isn't that much to do. A cleaning service comes once a week to take care of the heavy stuff, and my mother—"

"Your mother mentioned that she was going to be away for a while. A cruise?" Elizabeth was wondering how to tactfully explain that it wasn't the house Mrs. Ward was concerned about.

"Yes, that's right. But it's only a temporary situation—just a month or so. Did my mother explain that?"

"Oh yes," Elizabeth said. "She did indeed."

Life is short," Grace Ward had told her. "*My dear, I've always wanted to see the world, and I'm not getting any younger. If you work out as well as I think you're going to, then when this cruise is over, I might just hop a freighter and keep right on going!*"

"Well, I, frankly, I would think that in your situation, you'd be wanting something a little more permanent." Culley looked pointedly at Wendy, who flashed him a heartbreaker's smile from behind Elizabeth's legs.

Quite suddenly, Elizabeth knew that in spite of her situation she wanted very much to become Dr. G. Cullen Ward's housekeeper. Without being able to explain why, she knew that she felt good being here. She felt . . . right. The house needed her, Dr. Ward needed her. And the house was perfect for Wendy. The stone walls that made the estate seem so forbidding also made it a safe, secure place for a child to play. It was a nice area, and Dr. Ward was highly respected. Not even the Resnicks would be able to find fault with this environment.

Taking a deep breath, she said firmly, "Dr. Ward, for reasons I've discussed in full with your mother, but which I'd rather not go into right now"—she nodded meaningfully toward her daughter, who had ventured away from the sanctuary of her legs—"this job would suit my needs perfectly. Wendy and I are in urgent need of a place to live, and I need a job that will allow me to spend as much time as possible—"

"Live? You mean . . . *here?*"

Clearly, the fact that a live-in housekeeper usually does just that hadn't occurred to Dr. Ward. The look of consternation on his face would have made Elizabeth laugh, if winning his approval hadn't been so important. Instead she murmured tactfully, "Yes, of course, that was the arrangement as I discussed it with your mother."

The scientist's fingers made another destructive foray through his hair.

"She assured me you had plenty of room, even if you don't have maid's quarters, as such."

Culley shot her a distracted look. "Maid? Good Lord. No, no, it isn't that. It's just that this isn't exactly a house for children. I mean, it's . . . well, the stairs—"

With faultless timing, Wendy sang out, "Mommy, Mommy. Look at me!"

Both adults turned to stare at her. Near the top of the great curving staircase, Wendy was grinning at them through the balusters like a monkey through the bars of a cage.

"You were saying?" Elizabeth murmured, fighting back laughter.

Culley shot her a helpless frown. "Shouldn't you—won't she . . ."

Elizabeth sighed. She knew Wendy was in no danger of falling, but it wasn't a good time for a demonstration of typical two-year-old behavior either. Hoping for the best, she tried a coaxing tone. "Wendy, come back here. What are you doing up there, sweetheart?"

"Climbin'," Wendy announced, an intrepid expression on her face.

"Honey, this isn't Gramma's house. You come on back down now, okay?"

"No."

Culley's eyebrows went up. Elizabeth's heart sank. It was going to be one of *those* times.

Raising her voice to a no-nonsense level, she said, "Wendy, you come back here now."

Culley folded his arms on his chest and leaned against the newel post, looking expectant.

"Bye bye." With an impish wave, Wendy turned and continued on up the stairs.

Elizabeth muttered "Damn!" under her breath. There was a muffled sound from Culley. Suspecting that he was beginning to enjoy her discomfort, she threw him a look of exasperation. He gazed placidly back at her, his expression solemn, only a certain gleam in his eyes confirming her suspicions.

She shook her head and released her breath slowly. "I'm sorry, Dr. Ward. I guess she's going to be stubborn." Wendy, you little monster, don't do this to me—to us! You're blowing it!

Wendy had reached the top of the stairs and disappeared. Elizabeth cleared her throat. "Well, I guess I'd better go and . . ."

Culley straightened and gestured with exaggerated courtesy. "Please, by all means, be my guest."

Sighing in resignation, Elizabeth started up the stairs after her daughter. Without a word, Culley stuck his hands in his pockets and fell in beside her. Elizabeth glanced at him, swallowed, and said, "I'm really sorry. She's just at that age."

The scientist uttered a noncommittal "Hmm." He appeared to be deep in thought. Elizabeth studied his profile, searching for some sign there might still be hope he could be convinced to hire as his housekeeper a woman who couldn't even manage her own child. It didn't look promising. The profile was undeniably attractive, but the high forehead was furrowed, and the jaw and mouth were set in what looked like uncompromising lines.

To fill the silence, and to forestall the comments she knew must be straining the limits of his self-control, Elizabeth said, "You were a child in this house, weren't you?" Taking his grunt for confirmation, she went on, brightly, "I'll bet you had fun playing on these stairs . . . sliding down the banister."

This time the muffled sound he made was definitely one of amusement, and when he turned to look at her, a smile was tugging at one corner of his mouth, deepening the crease there. Again he had that engaging, boyish look. Elizabeth found herself afflicted with sudden shortness of breath and tightened her grip on the cherry wood banister.

"Yes," Culley said, "I suppose I did."

He paused in the middle of the staircase. One step above him Elizabeth did the same, bringing her to his eye level. Their eyes met in one of those rare moments of understanding between strangers that transcends verbal communication. For just a moment. And then he moved on and so did she, climbing the stairs side by side, at once more relaxed with each other and more aware.

"Goodness, how many bedrooms are there?" Elizabeth asked in dismay when they reached the top of the stairs and Wendy was nowhere in sight. A long hallway stretched ahead of her, with several open doors offering possibilities to tempt an inquisitive child. Her heart sank; Wendy's favorite game at the moment was hide-and-seek.

Culley was frowning again. "Six . . . no, seven." He shifted uncomfortably. "Listen, it's not that there isn't room for you and your daughter. Tell me honestly—can you imagine one little girl being happy in this mausoleum?"

Oh yes, Elizabeth could imagine one little girl being happy in this great stone house, with arched windows to let in the sunshine, a long banister to slide down, and a dozen rooms to play hide-and-seek in. Just as she could imagine one rather serious, very intelligent little boy being happy in this house. The fact was, she could imagine a whole troop of children laughing and roughhousing in the hallways. The house yearned for children.

When she didn't answer, Culley went on, speaking slowly, deliberately. "It isn't that I have anything against children. I don't. Really. But you see, I have my office upstairs, and I'm afraid that—"

"Your office? But I thought you worked at Cal Tech."

"I do. I do." His hand raked his hair into new disarray. "But I . . . um . . . I do research here. Experiments. Things like that. And I really need solitude for my work. Peace and quiet. I'm sorry, it's nothing personal to do with you or your daughter. She's a cute kid. But I just think—"

He was going to turn her down. She didn't know why she minded so much; surely there were other jobs, other solutions to her problems. If this didn't work out, she wasn't going to be out on the streets, for heaven's sake! But there was a lump in her throat the size of a golf ball.

"She's in bed by seven o'clock," Elizabeth said, trying to keep her voice from wobbling. "She wouldn't disturb your work, Dr. Ward, I promise. Please, just give me a chance. I . . . I really need this job."

Culley was staring down at his folded arms. Elizabeth followed his gaze and saw her own hands resting on his shirt sleeve. She could feel the firm warmth of muscle through the fabric. Her mouth dropped open, and so did his; but before either of them could comment, they heard a sound that transfixed them both.

From somewhere down the long hallway came the anguished sobbing of a heartbroken child.

Two

Culley moved first. He could feel adrenaline washing through his muscles like cold fire as he sprinted for the far end of the hall. Elizabeth was close behind him, so close that when he saw the little girl coming toward him and stopped suddenly, she ran right into him. And then, for some reason, she wrapped her arms around his waist and hung on, as if she thought she'd fall down if she let go. He could feel her body shaking.

In a high, scared voice she said, "Wendy! What is it, baby, what's the matter?"

The little girl's hood had fallen back, and strands of blond hair were stuck to her wet cheeks. Snuffling, trying now to control her sobs, she slowly lifted the thing she was carrying in her hands.

"Kitty . . . eat it," she wailed between hiccups. "Kitty *eat* it!"

Culley stared in disbelief at the slippery wet black kitten squirming in the child's hands and whispered, "Good God." The kitten's pink mouth opened to emit a tiny, raspy "Mew."

Elizabeth was already down on her knees in front of the distraught child, crooning words of reassurance. "It's all right, baby . . . here, let Mommy see, okay?"

"Kitty *eat* it!" Wendy insisted, her tone more indignant now than tragic.

"No, no, sweetheart—here, let Mommy have it—the kitty wasn't going to eat it. She was just washing it. Was she licking it? Like this? Yes? That's the way kitties wash their babies, honey, did you know that?"

Wendy gave a loud, skeptical sniff, clearly not buying it. Cradling the newborn kitten in her hands, Elizabeth looked up at Culley. It was one of those looks, one of those moments that goes whizzing by so quickly there isn't time to register its effect, until later it hits you with a double whammy, like a sonic boom. Right then all he saw was a heart-shaped Botticelli face haloed in red-gold and illuminated by so much love and laughter, joy and wonder, that it was like looking into the sun.

"Where—" he croaked, and had to stop for air.

Elizabeth nodded in understanding and turned back to her daughter. "Wendy, can you tell Mommy where you found the baby kitty?" Wendy nodded. With infinite patience her mother prodded, "Can you show me?"

Again Wendy nodded, sniffling. "I show you, 'kay?" Taking a firm grip on Elizabeth's forefinger, she began towing her toward Culley's bedroom.

Culley muttered, "Oh my God," and dove past them.

As he'd feared, there was Prissy, curled up right smack in the middle of his bedspread. At his intrusion she looked up briefly, then went back to nuzzling a second squirming, mewing bundle between her hind legs. Culley groaned, and put his hand over his eyes. "Oh for Pete's sake!"

Elizabeth was on her knees again, beside his bed this time, one arm around her daughter, pulling her close enough to see what was going on. "See?" she crooned in hushed tones, "the kitty's having babies, honey, isn't that wonderful?" Wendy gave an enthusiastic nod. "Look, see how the baby is all wet and yucky? The mother kitty has to lick him to make him nice and clean. Let's put this baby back now, so his mother can make him all clean, too, okay?"

Wendy nodded and said in a spellbound whisper, "Kitty wash it." Her daughter occupied for the moment, Elizabeth stood up, touched the back of her hand to her wet eyelashes and laughed softly. "What a surprise."

Culley let his breath out in a gust. "I'll say!"

Her eyes widened; it struck him that he'd never seen eyes so expressive. "You mean you weren't expecting this?"

He lifted his hand, palm out. "I swear I just thought she was *fat.*"

Laughter erupted from her and was guiltily stifled, as if she feared she'd committed an indiscretion in church. The laughter lingered in her voice, though, as she murmured, "Some scientist *you* are!"

"Yeah, well, I'm a nuclear physicist, dammit, not a vet!" Instantly contrite, Culley muttered, "Sorry."

But he was thinking that it just proved his point. Having a kid around all the time wouldn't work out. Among other things, he'd have to watch his language.

"Well," Elizabeth said, "what now?"

He took a step backward. "Hey, don't look at me." But she went on looking at him, expectantly. Feeling at a complete loss, he glanced again at the mess on his bed and drove his fingers through his hair. "Listen, this is way out of my field. I don't have any idea what . . ." He waved his hand helplessly.

With a distinct lack of compassion, Elizabeth asked, "Come on, didn't you have animals when you were a kid?"

Culley noticed that a dimple had appeared in one of her cheeks. "Oh sure—dogs, cats, the usual. But they were never allowed to . . . um . . ." It occurred to him that he ought to have taken care of that little detail himself. Because he felt guilty about it, he added peevishly, "The damn—darn cat isn't even mine."

Elizabeth's eyebrows rose, and her dimple deepened. "Oh really? She certainly seems to feel at home here."

Culley glowered at her. Who did she think she was, this woman, this irrepressible stranger, showing up on his doorstep unannounced, invading his house and his bedroom, making herself right at home, as if she *belonged?* He tried to find some way to blame this on her, tried at least to resist the teasing sparkle in her eyes. Instead, something inside him seemed to be growing lighter, as if he'd received an infusion of air bubbles.

Taking note of that phenomenon with mild astonishment, he said, "Actually, she belongs to Albert. He brought her home one day last spring."

"Albert?"

"Yeah, *my* cat. And from the looks of those kittens, the one responsible for this mess. Hey look," he added plaintively, "do you think we could at least get her off my *bed?*"

They both looked at the culprit in silence for a moment. Prissy ignored them, busily mothering her new babies, which as far as Culley could tell, still numbered only two. She also seemed to be ignoring Wendy, who had crawled up on the king-sized bed in order to get closer to the action.

"To be perfectly honest, I don't know all that much about it either. I was a child the last time this happened to me. But I don't think we ought to disturb her until we're sure she's finished and settled down, do you?"

As much as he hated the idea of what was happening to his bed, Culley thought she was probably right. "All right, so what do we do in the meantime? Does she . . . shouldn't we do something? Call the vet?"

"Oh, I don't think so." Elizabeth's smile hinted at

age-old feminine secrets, unfathomable to the masculine mind. "It looks as if she's doing very nicely without help. Cats have been doing this sort of thing for quite a while, you know." Culley made a noise of masculine frustration. Taking pity on him, Elizabeth patted his arm and said comfortingly, "We probably should keep an eye on her, just in case. And when we're sure she's finished, we'll find her a nice, cozy box."

"It's apt to be a while, I suppose," Culley said gloomily. It was becoming obvious that Princess Kerissa was going to have to endure one more night in dire circumstances while he played midwife to a cat. And then it occurred to him that since he was stuck with the situation anyway, he was very glad to have company. Suddenly inspired, he looked at Elizabeth and blurted, "Would you like some hot chocolate?"

"Hot chocolate? That would be—" A look of consternation replaced the smile on her face. "Oh gosh, I forgot. It must be getting late, it's got to be way past Wendy's bedtime. Wendy, honey—" She turned back toward the bed. Culley saw her shoulders sag, then lift again with her soft sigh. "Oh dear."

He moved up behind her, and together they looked down on the sleeping child. It made quite a picture: Little blond head pillowed on one curled fist, not two feet from the cat and her kittens.

"I guess I should have known she was being too quiet," Elizabeth whispered, with an odd little break in her voice.

Culley didn't say anything. Elizabeth's fine, red-gold hair was just about level with his chin. He noticed that it had a sunny citrus smell. As he inhaled deeply it struck him that if he lifted his chin a little bit, he could probably tuck her head right underneath it, which would mean, of course, that she'd be nestled against the front of him, and his arms would probably be around her. . . . Just a scientific observation, of course.

"Well," he said, clearing his throat, "since she's asleep anyway, what about that hot chocolate?"

She turned to face him, her lips parted, her eyes still reflecting the tenderness and love she was feeling right then for her child. She was very near, so near that Culley could see the tracings of freckles in her fair skin. He tried to find some scientific basis for that observation, and for the way his heartbeat was accelerating, but the analytical part of his mind seemed to have shut down.

Elizabeth murmured, "Oh, I don't—"

"She's asleep anyway. You might just as well stay and keep me company."

He barely caught the delicate sound she made as she cleared her throat. "All right." She cleared her throat again, moving back a step to put some distance between them. "I guess I might as well. But I think I ought to stay here, if you don't mind. In case Wendy wakes up. It's a strange place, and if I wasn't here . . ."

"I understand." And now for some reason he had to clear his throat, too. "Stay here, make yourself comfortable. I'll go get us some hot chocolate. Unless you'd rather have coffee?"

"Chocolate's fine." She was smiling again. Culley took the memory of her smile with him down the stairs, through the quiet hallways, and into the big empty kitchen.

Albert was curled up in his favorite place on the counter. Culley gave him a dirty look and muttered, "Yeah, look what you've gotten me into, *pal*." The cat opened one eye, gave him a baleful yellow stare, and went back to sleep.

When he got back upstairs with two big mugs of chocolate, he found Elizabeth curled up on his bed beside her daughter. For an instant he thought she'd gone to sleep, too, but when she heard him she lifted her head and then started to get up, as if she felt guilty about being caught lying there.

He whispered, "No, no, stay put," and held out one of the mugs. He was surprised by how much he liked the look of her there. She reminded him of a painting, a Renoir, maybe—red-gold hair and porcelain skin against the deep, masculine tones of his bed-spread.

Who was she, he wondered, and where had his mother found her? It seemed almost unbelievable that this lovely woman had come knocking on his door on Halloween night to talk about a job as his *housekeeper*. She sure didn't look like anyone's idea of a housekeeper. She was so small and slender, with an air of fragility and softness that made her seem little more than a child herself; and yet, there was a certain something about the set of her mouth and chin, something in her eyes when she gazed at her child. Courage, heart . . . Culley wasn't sure what it was, but it made him think of a lioness, ready to defend her cub against all comers.

She raised herself on her elbow and took the cup from him, smiling a little when she saw the marsh-mallows. "She had another one while you were gone," she informed him, blowing on her cocoa. "This one's got some white spots."

Culley said, "Hmm." He was willing to take her word that there was another kitten. He was too ab-sorbed with enjoying the sight of her poking the bob-bing marshmallows with her finger, watching her take a cautious sip, then lick sticky white foam from her upper lip. . . .

He sat down on the foot of his bed with his back to her. There was silence while they both sipped the hot cocoa.

"Good," Elizabeth said after a moment.

"Don't sound so surprised." Culley's smile was wry; he knew exactly what she was thinking. "In spite of what my mother may have told you, I'm not com-pletely inept." When she didn't comment, he added with dry amusement, "She thinks I need a keeper.

But I suppose she told you that. Actually, I'm just a bit . . . forgetful."

Her voice sounded suspiciously muffled. "Oh really? I hadn't noticed."

"Yeah, well, I am," Culley said placidly. "Nothing serious—I just forget where I'm supposed to be, from time to time, and where I put things."

He heard the ripple of her laughter. "Like the fork?"

Culley hitched himself around to look at her. "I beg your pardon?"

"Never mind."

He frowned. "May I ask you a question?"

"Sure."

Her one-word reply was spontaneous, trusting, generous. As she was, he realized. "Why would somebody like you want to keep house for somebody like me?"

He saw her swallow. Her gaze shifted downward, avoiding his. "What do you mean, 'someone like me'?"

The way she said it, he wasn't sure which part of the question she wanted clarified. Because he didn't feel like defining himself, he chose the simpler interpretation. "You're young, attractive, intelligent . . ."

". . . single, and a parent," she finished with a sardonic little smile.

"Ah." He glanced at her ringless hands, curved around the cocoa mug, and ventured, "Divorced?"

She shook her head. "Widowed."

"I'm sorry." His voice was husky. Empathy wrapped him in its cocoon of pain, both shared and remembered.

"It's all right," she said. "It's been a year and a half." Her voice was entirely without emotion. Her lashes came down like a curtain.

"Still," he murmured, wondering about that, and about the brittleness in her voice, and the slight tightening around her mouth. Then he was surprised to hear himself volunteer, "It's been five years for me, and it's still hard."

Her eyes flashed to his face.

He said softly, "Didn't my mother tell you?"

"She mentioned that your wife had died, but . . ." She left it hanging, clearly uncomfortable with the subject.

"It was cancer, a particularly virulent kind. It happened very quickly." He paused. "And your husband?"

"Accident." Her manner was distant, the word as clipped and final as hanging up on a telephone call.

As he made conventional noises of sympathy, Culley was experiencing what were, for him, some very unconventional feelings. The moment of empathy had passed, and instead he was feeling shut out and frustrated, the way he did when the answer to a scientific question eluded him. He was curious about this woman, but the more he tried to find out about her, the more distance there seemed to be between them.

"So," he asked, disguising his probing behind the flat, disinterested tones of casual conversation, "what have you been doing for the last year? For a job and a place to live, I mean."

She shrugged, relaxing only slightly, and leaned across his bed to place her empty cup on his nightstand. It was a subtle evasion. "I've been living with my in-laws."

"Ah," Culley said, nodding. "I see." He asked no more questions, because he did see. Elizabeth's words were like a stone skipping across a pond, barely riffling its surface; Cully instantly felt he knew all that was hidden in the quiet depths of the pond.

It took considerably less intelligence and imagination than Culley possessed to grasp the financial realities a young, single woman would face, trying to earn a living and raise a small child alone. Even with a college degree, on the average starting salary, by the time she paid for rent and child care, there wouldn't be much left over for even the bare necessities. And even more clearly than the arithmetic of the situation, Culley could visualize what it must be like for a working mother to see her child only for a few hours a day, to know that another woman was soothing her hurts and fears and experiencing all those precious baby "firsts." He could certainly understand why, under the circumstances, Elizabeth might have chosen her in-laws' hospitality and support.

And he also understood why she would want to get out from under it. He'd seen pride and determination in those gray-green eyes of hers, as well as fierce maternal devotion—that look of the lioness. She was a fighter. He really had to admire her courage.

But when he turned to gaze at her again he felt momentarily off balance, as if he'd taken a confident step, only to encounter an unexpected wrinkle in the path.

Because right now she didn't look much like a lioness.

He didn't know how long he'd been silent; as usual, when deep in thought, he'd lost all track of time. But while he'd been ruminating, Elizabeth had fallen asleep. She was lying on her side, one arm pillowing her head, the other thrown protectively across her child's body. Wendy snored softly; Elizabeth's breathing was silent, deep, and even. A few inches away the mother cat lay with her eyes closed, purring, while her newborn kittens slept curled close against her belly.

Culley watched them for a long time. He noticed that Elizabeth was wearing a soft heather-gray sweater with a plain round neckline. It occurred to him that it would match her eyes, and he wondered why he hadn't noticed that before. But she'd had on a coat, he remembered—something belted, like a trenchcoat. It was there on the chair by the window, along with Wendy's Red Riding Hood cape. Her sunset cloud of hair had tumbled back onto the bed-spread, revealing one small, delicate ear, and an ear-ring shimmering like a raindrop on the petal of a flower.

He felt an urge to touch her, followed by a wave of longing as unexpected as it was intense. He was so shaken he got to his feet, and from that safer distance stood looking down at them—mother, child, cat, and kittens, all asleep in the middle of *his* bed.

After a long time, he picked up the edge of his bed-spread, drew it carefully over the sleeping woman and child, and went out, leaving a single lamp burning.

Elizabeth felt comfortable, lying with the cat's purring in her ears, Wendy's moist breath on her arm, wrapped in the warm cocoon of bedspread.

She blinked open her eyes to subdued golden light and looked around. Why hadn't Culley awakened her and sent her home? Instead, he had tucked his bedspread around her and gone quietly away, leaving his own bed to a cat and a couple of strangers. She closed her eyes again and thought of Dr. G. Cullen Ward, asleep somewhere in that big, silent house, his glasses on the nightstand, dark lashes making crescent shadows on slack cheeks; jaws stubbled, hair falling too long across his forehead, mouth relaxed, vulnerable. He must be a kind man, she thought, as deep inside her a small vibration began, almost as if she felt the cat's purring in her own chest.

She knew she should get out of bed, pick up Wendy, and go. But, she argued, she didn't have any idea what time it was, or how long she'd slept, and if she disturbed Wendy now, she'd probably never get her back to sleep again. And what would her in-laws say when she came dragging in at God knows what hour, with poor little Wendy still in her Halloween costume? She'd never hear the end of it!

Even wrapped in the heavy woven spread, with her daughter's heated body against hers, Elizabeth felt a chill. She could just see the Resnicks' disapproving eyes, hear their criticisms, so thinly disguised as questions or suggestions. Oh, how she dreaded going back there, for even one more day, one more night!

She thought of her room, and Wendy's right next door, done especially for them in shades of lavender, coral, and pink. Margaret had hired a professional decorator, of course, sparing no expense because, as she so often reminded Elizabeth, she and Wendy were all they had left of Kevin now.

Perhaps, Elizabeth thought, as she often did, lying wakeful in the dark and lonely hours, if they *had* spared some of the expense and all of the criticism, and spent more of warmth and love and acceptance, maybe their handsome, intelligent, talented son would have liked himself better. Maybe, she thought, he'd have liked himself enough to accept *her* love. And maybe he'd have liked himself enough to keep away from the drugs that had already destroyed his mind and body and completely killed that love, long before he'd pumped his system full of drugs one last time and driven his motorcycle into a tree.

But it was pointless to think about that now. She'd made up her mind a long time ago not to give in to bitterness and anger. She was strong, as Kevin hadn't been. She was a survivor. She *would* make a place in this world for herself and Wendy, a safe and happy place. A loving place.

But as she let her eyes roam around the room, touching soft fabrics, drinking in the warmth of earth tones and old wood, resting on the comfortable clutter of well-thumbed books and lived-in clothing, Elizabeth felt a wistful kind of yearning. Like a wayfarer warming her hands before a fire, or a lost child enfolded in comforting arms, she wished it were possible to somehow stay here, just like this, forever . . . safe, secure, and cherished.

Culley woke with the sun in his eyes. It was exactly what he deserved, he thought, for choosing one of the east bedrooms. Actually, the one he'd ended up in, probably out of habit, was his old room, the one he'd slept in throughout his childhood. All of his stuff had been cleared out years ago, of course, but it still had the same wallpaper—beige and navy blue, with ships, tall-masted sailing ships, clippers, barques, schooners, and galleons. He'd always liked that wallpaper.

The bed was something else. It was a twin, for one thing, which he wasn't used to, and he hadn't bothered to make it up, but had just slept in his clothes on top of the mattress with the bedspread for a blanket. As a consequence, he felt stiff and rumpled and badly in need of a shower.

He frowned as he stretched, thinking that a shower was going to present a problem. Like a lot of older houses, his was long on beds, short on bathrooms. There were only two—one at each end of the hall. The one closest to this room was his mother's; his was clear down at the other end of the hall, across from his room. He supposed he could use his mother's bathroom, but all his stuff was in the other one. Not to mention the fact that his clothes were in his room, which had lately been taken over by cats and strangers.

With a yawn and a groan, Culley got up and padded barefooted into the hallway. It was very quiet, which surprised him. He'd pretty much resigned himself to being wakened by the patter of little feet this morning; he'd had an idea two-year-olds would be early risers.

Damn, he thought. How was he going to get to his clean clothes without disturbing his uninvited guests?

He could probably tiptoe in and out in his bare feet, but opening up his dresser drawers would wake them for sure.

A picture came unanticipated into his mind, a vivid, technicolor image of Elizabeth, hair mussed, cheeks flushed, opening her eyes and smiling up at him from his pillows. It did interesting things to his breathing.

Whoa, he thought, laughing at himself. He always had been somewhat of a morning person. Memories flooded him—memories of Shannon and him, rolling and tumbling like puppies in sun-warmed sheets, laughing and protesting to each other, without much conviction, that they couldn't . . . shouldn't . . . not *now* . . . they simply must get up and get ready for work.

Gently but firmly, Culley put the memories away. The past was past; nothing could ever bring Shannon back. The present was waiting for him now in his bedroom, and he couldn't put off dealing with it any longer. He needed a shower, and he needed clean clothes. He wanted his room back. Enough was enough.

Resolutely, he strode down the hall to his room, lifted his hand and knocked on the door.

There was no answer. Slowly, cautiously, Culley turned the doorknob, pushed open the door, and stuck his head inside.

The room was empty.

Three

They were gone, all of them, Elizabeth, Wendy, cat, and kittens. His bed was bare, stripped to the mattress, except for the pillows, which lay caseless and askew against the headboard. Culley began to feel a little like that himself, askew, out of place, in the Twilight Zone.

Then he noticed the box on the floor in the corner of the room. In it, on something that looked a lot like one of his oldest and most beloved sweatshirts, the three kittens lay draped across each other like limp black and white sausages, sound asleep. Their mother was nowhere around.

Culley looked at the kittens, then at his bed, and uttered a soft and wondering "Huh!"

So they were gone. His life was back on track, running along familiar grooves. Well, he told himself, thank goodness for that. He had important things to do, alpha particles to track, new space systems to design . . . a princess to rescue.

And his bedroom and bathroom were his again; no reason why he couldn't just shuck off his rumpled clothes and jump in the shower. Somehow, though, it didn't seem as urgent to him as it had only moments before. He decided he'd better go downstairs instead. Prissy was probably looking for something to eat after her night's labors, and if he didn't feed her, no telling what she'd get into.

Halfway down the stairs he thought he smelled coffee. His heart rate and footsteps accelerated, but he didn't admit to himself the reason for it. Nor did he acknowledge the uplift in his spirits when he heard voices coming from the other side of the kitchen door. But when he walked in and saw them there, he couldn't deny the fact that he was glad to see them, and that what he'd felt mostly when he'd thought they'd gone was disappointment.

Elizabeth was standing at the counter, squeezing oranges. Culley stopped just inside the door and let the sight of her pour over him like morning sunshine. She'd shoved the sleeves of her sweater above her elbows. He noticed how slender her arms looked, how small her hands were. He marveled at the strength in them as they deftly pressed and twisted the orange halves on the old-fashioned hand juicer. He noticed that with the morning sun shining through it, her hair seemed only a shade or two darker than the fruit.

Wendy was lying on her stomach on the floor near her mother's feet, busily scribbling in a coloring book with a purple crayon. When she saw Culley she stopped what she was doing and crowed, "Daddy!"

Turning to give him a wry and apologetic smile, Elizabeth murmured, "No, no, baby, remember what I told you? That's Dr. Ward." Her voice had a certain huskiness in it that awakened dormant memories in Culley . . . memories of "Good Morning" spoken with a sense of loving wonder amidst tangled sheets.

"Doctah Word?" Wendy repeated without conviction.

Culley didn't pay much attention to her, and neither did Elizabeth. She murmured "Good morning," and then just went on looking at him, smiling that shy, uncertain smile, touching back a wisp of her hair with the back of her hand. She'd pulled it into a ponytail and fastened it with a rubber band, but that didn't keep tendrils of it from wafting around her face like errant, windblown flames.

Mumbling a vague " 'Morning . . ." in return, he went over to her, ostensibly to get a better look at what she was doing, but mostly because her warmth drew him, like a fire on a cold morning.

"I hope it's all right," she said, flicking an uncertain glance at the oranges. "When I went to let the cat outside I saw the tree right there beside the back door, and they looked so good, and I thought you might like—"

He cut her off with an impatient gesture. "Of course it's okay. Pick as many as you like, that's what they're for." He felt vaguely annoyed, as if something important had been interrupted by something petty and mundane. And then he felt ridiculous. Heaven knew the oranges needed picking, and he did enjoy fresh-squeezed juice. He smiled. "In fact, if you've got an extra glass, it looks great."

"Oh!" She gave an embarrassed sounding laugh and handed him a tall, moisture-beaded glass. "Here, this is yours. I, um, made some coffee, too, if you . . ." Her voice trailed off.

Culley drank down the juice like a thirsty man, tilting back his head and closing his eyes. When he opened them again, he found her watching him, looking slightly dazed. When he licked the tart-sweet traces of juice from his lips and swallowed, her eyes followed those minute movements of mouth and throat as if mesmerized by them.

He said, "That's good," and found that his throat felt dry.

Elizabeth's eyes flicked up to meet his for one startled moment, then slid away. "Wendy helped pick," she said brightly. "Didn't you, baby?"

Wendy confirmed that with a nod, then announced grandly, "I'm coloring!"

As Culley shifted his gaze from mother to daughter, he wondered about the funny little unease that seemed to spring up between him and Elizabeth. It was odd . . . definitely not the usual awkwardness of strangers.

Wendy was holding up her coloring book for his inspection. He glanced at it, then shoved his glasses back into place with a forefinger and raised one eyebrow at Elizabeth. "Solar the Antarian?"

Elizabeth shrugged; she was squeezing oranges again. "It was the one she picked."

"Isn't it a little . . . sophisticated for a two-year-old? I mean, all those alien bad guys."

"*She* doesn't know they're bad guys," Elizabeth said matter-of-factly, "and she sees worse looking things on *The Muppet Show.* You want to know something?" She turned to smile at him over her shoulder. "Personally, I love Solar the Antarian."

"You do?"

"Yeah, I really do. I can't wait for the third movie in the trilogy. I think it's supposed to be out next summer. He's like . . . kind of a cross between Robin Hood and the Lone Ranger, you know? And maybe Captain Kirk. There's something about him that definitely reminds me of the old-time heroes. I think the person who created him must be a real romantic. What's his name—Wardlaw? Something something Wardlaw, I can't remember the initials. I've never seen him interviewed, but I'll bet he's a very interesting person."

"Hmm," Culley said, frowning intently down at Wendy, who was tugging on his pants leg and chanting, "Color me, Daddy, color me, Daddy."

"She want's you to color *with* her," Elizabeth explained, touching her forehead distractedly with the back of her hand. "Um . . . look, Wendy, Dr. Ward can't color with you. He's busy, honey. And anyway, it's time for breakfast. Here's your orange juice. Come sit in the chair now."

"Cooperative this morning," Culley commented dryly as Wendy abandoned her crayons without argument and climbed into the chair her mother was holding.

Elizabeth glanced at him. He found himself gazing at the pink in her cheeks and thinking that a woman's blush was a very interesting physical phenomenon.

"Look, Dr. Ward, I hope you know how sorry I am about . . . everything. I'm so sorry about your bed—"

"Listen, forget it. It wasn't your fault." Culley shrugged. All of a sudden he was feeling very mellow.

"But I—Wendy and I . . . Dr. Ward, I don't know why I did that. I don't know what made me fall asleep like that, I've never . . . We put you out. I'm really sorry."

"It's all right," Culley murmured, "I found a place to sleep."

"I'm washing your blankets and everything. But I'm afraid the spread should be sent to the cleaners. I'll pay for it—"

"Why? *You* didn't have kittens in my bed." Still smiling, he looked at Wendy, and found her beaming back at him through an orange juice mustache.

"Want some, Daddy?" She tilted her head winsomely. "It's good juice."

From Elizabeth's direction came a small sound of vexation. She muttered, "I don't know why she keeps doing that. I've tried to explain. She was just a tiny baby when my—when her father died, and she doesn't understand. She thinks all men are daddies. Dr. Ward, I—"

"*Culley,*" he said harshly, his mellow mood evaporated.

Elizabeth opened her mouth, closed it, and looked around distractedly, as if seeking escape. "We should go. You probably—I just waited because I didn't want to leave without a chance to thank you, and I wanted to apologize for all the inconvenience we caused you, and tell you about your sheets and things."

Culley took a deep breath. She didn't understand, of course. Why should she? Making an effort to mask the emotions she'd unwittingly dredged up in him, he raked his hand through his hair and let his breath out slowly and carefully.

"How about this. Why don't you both call me Culley? Would that help?" When she still looked confused he tried a smile, and felt it slip awry. "It's what nearly everyone calls me—short for G. Cullen. And yes, the G stands for Gregory, which no one in the world, except the woman responsible for it, *ever* calls me. And if you ever call me that, I'll fire you on the spot."

There was a little silence. Then Elizabeth shook her head and whispered, "I don't . . . think I understand."

"What don't you understand?"

"Does this mean—are you *hiring* me?"

Culley nodded. The spasm of pain had passed, like a very small black cloud that only momentarily blocks the sun. And just as the sunshine seems to feel even sweeter after such an eclipse, he was suddenly feeling so mellow he wanted to hug somebody or to burst into song.

"If you still want it, I guess the job is yours. As long as you understand that it's temporary. Just until Grace—until my mother gets back from her cruise."

"Oh, I understand," she said quickly, in a low, tense voice. Culley noticed that her hand had come to rest on Wendy's head, an unconscious gesture of maternal protectiveness. It piqued his curiosity. He thought he understood why she wanted this job for her own sake, but what did it have to do with Wendy?

He started to say, "When can you start?" just as she said, "When do you want me—?" and they both stopped, laughing self-consciously.

Culley said, "Anytime. The sooner the better."

Elizabeth said, "Okay, well, I need to go home and . . ."

"I understand. That's fine. Tomorrow, then?"

"*No.* No. I can come back later today. If that's all right?"

"Yeah, okay, that's fine. If I'm not home yet, just—wait a minute, I've got a spare house key somewhere." He felt as nervous as a kid making a date for the prom. But then, he told himself, he'd never hired a housekeeper before. Or anyone else, for that matter. He thought vaguely that there probably were questions he should be posing, references he should be asking for, or some such things. But none of that seemed relevant, after the night just past, and the odd intimacy they'd shared. He felt as if he'd known Elizabeth for years. And besides, he reassured himself, his mother had probably taken care of everything, as she usually did.

Miraculously, he found the extra key in the drawer beside the refrigerator, right where it belonged. As he handed it to Elizabeth, he noticed that her eyes seemed very bright, and that her fingers, when she took it from him, seemed to shake. He noticed the small convulsion in her slender throat just before she murmured, "Thank you. You won't regret this, I promise."

He didn't know what to say to that, so he just shrugged and said briskly, "Well then. I guess that's it. Oh, you can decide which rooms would suit you and Wendy. I'll leave that up to you. So . . . unless you have any questions?" She shook her head. "Okay, then, I guess I'd better get showered and . . ." Halfway to the door he remembered something and turned back. "The cat, Prissy. Is everything all right?"

She nodded. "She's fine. I let her out. Will she—?"

"She uses the cat doors. You'll notice they're all over the house, so you don't have to worry about her. I'll just have to remember to leave my bedroom door open." He gave her a wry smile. "I *will* remember, I promise. So, I guess I'll see you this evening. Right?"

Elizabeth said faintly, "Right."

As he turned back to the door, Wendy sang out, "Bye, Daddy!" Culley went out, thinking that this arrangement was going to take some getting used to. He wondered why he didn't find the prospect distressing; why, in fact, he felt a sense of light-hearted anticipation, like a kid waiting in line for the Ferris wheel.

"Where'sa man goin'?" Wendy asked her mother.

"To work, baby," Elizabeth said absently, gazing at the closing door.

"Why?"

"Because that's what—" She jerked her eyes and her attention back to her daughter just in time. She'd almost said, "Because that's what daddies do." Whatever Wendy had where this man was concerned, it seemed to be contagious!

And dangerous. It was one thing for Wendy to call him Daddy, since he didn't seem to mind it. In time Wendy would learn the difference between *man* and *daddy*, and in the meantime, Dr. Ward would provide a more than acceptable father figure, something that had been sorely lacking in her daughter's life up to now. But it would be quite another thing if she were to allow him to assume any place in her own mind except that of *employer*. Period. And she had a feeling that might not be hard to do. Dr. G. Cullen Ward was a lot younger and more attractive than Elizabeth had anticipated, and as his housekeeper, she knew that a certain amount of close personal contact was going to be unavoidable. For the first time it occurred to her that she was going to be doing this man's laundry, making his bed, picking up after him, cooking his meals, shopping for him. In short, doing all the things a wife would do, except one.

Her mind shied away from that thought like a skittish horse jumping at a butterfly.

"What'sa matter, Mommy?"

"Nothing, baby," Elizabeth muttered, observing a strange, quivery feeling just below her ribs.

Wendy's next question was a breathless, "What's that?" as a loud thump came from out in the main hallway.

"I don't know." With a puzzled frown Elizabeth pushed open the door.

Culley was standing at the bottom of the staircase, frozen in a sort of half crouch, with one foot on the first step, one hand on the newel post. At Elizabeth's unexpected intrusion, his head came up, and his eyes met hers in a look that was startled, and, she could have sworn, *guilty.*

"What?" he asked, sounding slightly testy and out of breath.

Elizabeth said, "I heard a noise. I thought—it sounded like something fell. Are you all right?"

"Oh, fine . . . fine. No, I was just . . . everything's fine. No problem." Elizabeth watched fascinated while he arranged his features in dignified lines, valiantly ignoring a deepening flush. And all at once understanding dawned. Delight woke and stirred inside her like a newborn butterfly.

Culley made a sound like a cough. "Was there something you needed?"

"Oh no," Elizabeth hastened to assure him, keeping a straight face with difficulty. "Everything's fine."

"Well then, I'll see you this evening."

"Yes. I'll be here."

As she returned to the kitchen and Wendy's inevitable questions, she was still struggling to quell that swelling effervescence that precedes an eruption of laughter. Because, as unlikely as it seemed, Elizabeth *knew* beyond any doubt that her new employer, Dr. G. Cullen Ward, world-renowned scientist and future Nobel prize winner, had just slid down the banister.

Wendy didn't want to leave. She liked the house. She liked lying on her tummy on the floor in a warm patch of sunshine with her coloring book and crayons, while her mommy made happy, humming noises above her. She liked helping to pick oranges, and she liked the way the big doors all had little tiny doors in them, just the right size for her to squeeze through. She liked the great big stairs and sleeping in a great big bed with her mommy's arms around her. She liked the baby kitties, the way they squirmed and tickled against her neck.

She'd wanted to go up the stairs and pet the kittens one more time, just to say good-bye, but Mommy had said no, they had to go back to Grandma's house now. Wendy didn't want to go back to Grandma's house. She'd let Mommy know how much she wanted to stay and see the kitties, and how much she didn't want to go to Grandma's house, but it hadn't done any good. Mommy had just picked her up and carried her outside and strapped her into her car seat, and there wasn't anything Wendy could do about it but let her feelings out, *loudly.*

"Hush, Wendy," her mother said. "Do you want Dr. Ward to hear you throwing a fit?"

Wendy sniffed and gulped and thought about that. Dr. Ward was the man, the daddy. She liked him, too. He was big and tall—taller than Mommy—and he smelled nice. And when he talked, it made a nice, fuzzy feeling inside her.

She sniffled again and shook her head. "No."

"Baby, it's only for a little while, and then we're coming back. But first we have to go to Grandma's house and get all of our clothes, and your toys, and your blankie. And then, you know what? We're going to come back and live here, and you can play with the kitties any time you want. Would you like that?"

That made Wendy feel happy and bubbly. She nodded, giggled, and said, "*Yeah.*"

Wendy's mother got into the car and started up the motor, but instead of moving, the car just sat there. After a while, Wendy's mother put her head back and closed her eyes and whispered, "Oh God. I did it." And then she wiped her cheeks with her hand.

Wendy got a bad feeling inside her, a lonesome, scared feeling, as if she wanted to cry, but couldn't. She said, "Mommy's cryin'. Why you sad, Mommy?"

Her mother looked at her and smiled. She touched Wendy's cheek, and the bad feelings inside her went away. "Oh, baby, it's okay. I'm not sad, I'm happy. I'm happy because you're my little girl, and I love you, and we're going to come and live here in this wonderful house, and you can run and play and pick oranges and play with kitties—"

"And *Daddy*," Wendy added, decisively.

Her mother said, "Oh, Wendy," and laughed.

The car began to move. Wendy turned around in her seat and watched until she couldn't see the house anymore. Then she whispered, "Bye-bye, house . . . bye-bye, kitties . . . bye-bye, Daddy," and facing front once more, began to think about going to Grandma's house. And she didn't feel happy anymore.

Wendy didn't like Grandma's house. It had lots of pretty things in it, but she wasn't allowed to touch them. The back yard was big, but it didn't have trees, just a swimming pool and some cement. That was good for riding her tricycle, but she wasn't allowed to go outside unless a grown-up was with her, because she might fall in the pool and drown. Wendy didn't know what that meant, but it didn't sound good. And she couldn't ride her tricycle in the house either, or run, or shout, or sing loud, because Grandma had headaches.

Wendy didn't like Grandma very much either. She knew she was supposed to like her, because Grandma liked her—a *lot*. But Grandma made her feel funny inside. Her voice was high and sharp, not soft, like Mommy's. She smelled all right, but sometimes she made Wendy's nose feel like she had a bad cold, and she hugged *too tight*.

But mostly Wendy didn't like Grandma because of the way Mommy looked when she was around. When Grandma was around, Mommy's face looked different. And her voice sounded different. She didn't know why, but when Mommy looked and sounded like that, Wendy felt scared.

Wendy looked over at her mother. Yep, Mommy's cheeks had that look again. Wendy turned and stared out the window at the cars and palm trees and tall, tall buildings and tried not to think about Grandma anymore. Maybe, she thought, Grampa Carl would be there, and it wouldn't be so bad. She liked Grampa Carl okay. He had a nice deep voice. Not as nice as the daddy's, though, and he didn't smell as nice as the daddy either. . . .

Wendy thought about the man Mommy called Dr. Ward, and after a while she forgot all about Grandma and began to smile.

"Mother Resnick, Maggie, please don't do that. I'm *not* trying to take Wendy away from you. That isn't—"

"Well, I certainly don't know what else you could be thinking of!"

Wendy tugged on Elizabeth's arm. "Mommy—"

"In a minute, baby. It isn't that far, Maggie, it's just right over the hill, not more than half an hour by freeway. You can—"

"Mommy, I have to go potty."

"And that's another thing! Los Angeles? What can

you be thinking of, moving a child right into downtown! That's no place for a baby!"

"It isn't downtown. It's—" Elizabeth stopped and pressed her lips together. She'd almost fallen for the trap and given away more information that she wanted to. "It's a very nice, old, residential neighborhood," she said placatingly. "Very quiet and safe."

"Mommy, I have to go *potty.*"

"Then go on and *go,* Wendy. You can do it by yourself."

"I don't understand," Margaret Resnick wailed, lifting her hands for added dramatic effect, "how you can just *leave,* all of a sudden like this, without any warning! You know how much we love you and Wendy. That child is the most important thing in the world to me, and I simply cannot understand how you can *do* this to me, after all we've done for you!"

"No I *can't,*" Wendy insisted, looking mulish.

Elizabeth gave her daughter a distracted glance. "It's not all of a sudden," she said doggedly, rubbing her eyes. "I told you when we moved in that it would only be until I found a job and a place to live. It's been more than a year since—"

"Carl, do something," Margaret demanded, cutting Elizabeth off before she could utter Kevin's name, or mention the accident. "Are you going to let her take our little girl away?"

It was Margaret's way—when the tears and histrionics and laying on of the heavy guilt trip failed, bring on the heavy artillery. Elizabeth sighed with resignation and girded for the real battle.

"No, Maggie, aren't you forgetting something? Wendy's not *our* little girl, she's Elizabeth's." Until now, Carl Resnick had been standing by the fireplace, meticulously tending his pipe, keeping out of things. But Elizabeth knew that both his attitude and his words were deceptive; Carl had his own methods of controlling, and Elizabeth knew he'd been listening carefully to everything, planning his strategy. Now as he came strolling unhurriedly across the room to look down at her through a curling plume of smoke, she couldn't control an inner cringe. His look was benevolent, and supremely self-confident, his CEO's look. "And our son's, of course. . . ."

"Mom-*mee!*" Wendy demanded, yanking on Elizabeth's unresponsive arm. "I . . . have . . . to . . . go . . . *potty!*"

"Liz, honey, naturally we're concerned about our only grandchild. We want to be sure she's happy . . . safe . . . well taken care of. Now, you know I've always told you, if there's anything you or Wendy need, all you have to do is ask."

Elizabeth could feel the muscles in her jaws growing tense. "I know, and that's . . . very kind of you. But . . ." *But I have to get on with my life! How can I have a life of my own while I remain in your house, a living shrine to your son's memory?* Aloud, struggling for an attitude of calm and authority, she said, "But Wendy is my responsibility, and I . . . I just think it's time I . . ." Her voice trailed off. Carl had sat down in a chair opposite her and was nodding sagely at his pipe.

"Well, that's certainly a commendable attitude, and I admire you for it, honey. I do." He leaned forward suddenly, his hands cupped around the pipe, elbows resting on his knees. "I'm sure you've given this a great deal of thought—all the financial ramifications?"

"Yes," Elizabeth said firmly, "I have."

"For instance . . ." Carl drawled casually, leaning over to place his pipe in an ashtray, "I assume this job has an adequate health insurance plan?"

Caught off-guard, Elizabeth could only mumble stupidly, "Health insurance?"

Her father-in-law's gaze snapped back to her, eyebrows raised. "Well sure, honey. You know I've always covered you and Wendy under my own policy, but I don't see how I can continue to justify doing that, do you? When I don't even know where you're going to be living?"

In the silence following that salvo, Wendy began to whimper. Elizabeth barely heard her. She could feel her face settling into a stubborn scowl. Why did Carl Resnick always seem to have the power to reduce her to the behavioral level of an intractable child?

"I'm going to take care of that," she said through clenched jaws.

"Good . . . good. I'm sure you will. Now, this man—this Dr. Ward. Of course, I'm going to have to have you give me more information about him—"

"Carl," Margaret put in, her tone aggrieved and her expression tragic, "she doesn't even want to give us her address! I can't understand *why*, after all we've done—"

"Now, Liz, I think that's being a little bit unreasonable, don't you? Obviously, before I let Wendy go and live with some stranger, I'll have to have him thoroughly checked out. I'll need to know his full name, address, place of employment—"

At that moment, while Elizabeth was struggling to hold back her own mounting frustration, Wendy wailed, *"Mom-meee,"* burst into tears, and wet the living room rug.

"Hello, Mother," Culley said into the telephone. "This is a surprise."

"What is? You knew I'd be calling. Tell me—"

"Where are you? This is a terrible connection. Is that mariachi music I hear in the background?"

"Cabo San Lucas. And yes, that is mariachi music. One hears a lot of that down here. What I really want—"

"How are you enjoying your cruise? You haven't gotten seasick, have you? I hear the weather's been—"

"Gregory, stop being annoying. You know very well why I called. I want to know what you think of her."

"Of who?"

"Of Elizabeth, of course! Have you hired her?"

Culley said blandly, "Ah, yes, Elizabeth. The housekeeper. Yes, as a matter of fact, I did hire her. On a temporary basis of course, only until you get back. I made that clear to her."

"Oh good. However there is one small thing."

"What?"

"How is she working out, by the way? You do like her? Everything's all right?"

"Yes. Well, actually, I don't really know. She moved in today. I don't even know if she can cook. So far, she's left me a sandwich for dinner." Culley looked at the piece of paper in his hand and grinned wryly. "And a note."

"What? Gregory, I can hardly hear you, you're going to have to speak up. Better yet, just listen. I did want to tell you that it might be a good idea not to set any specific dates with Elizabeth about exactly how long her services will be required. I may be gone a little longer than I originally planned. There's this wonderful cruise to Tahiti that would dovetail very nicely with this one, and as long as you have reliable help, well, you know how I've always wanted to go to Tahiti."

"Tahiti," Culley said under his breath, and then shrugged. He supposed it was to be expected; his mother was probably overdue for a mid-life crisis. Besides, it had been a long time since his father's last, and fatal, heart attack. "That's fine, Mom," he said gamely into the telephone. "Have a great time. Any idea how long you'll be gone?"

"Oh, I don't know," his mother said, her voice coming across the wires to the raucous accompaniment of laughter and mariachis. "Since I'll already be so close, I might just go on down to Australia . . .

New Zealand. Who knows? Maybe I'll even hop on over to Singapore! Gregory, I really must go. Everyone's waiting for me. I'm so glad you're getting along well with Elizabeth. Say hello for me, won't you? And kiss that darling little girl of hers for me too! Bye-bye, love. Take care of yourself."

Culley cradled the receiver and addressed it in tones of shocked disbelief: "*Singapore?*"

Actually, his feelings about this new development were mixed. On the one hand, he was delighted his mother was finding new interests and having such a good time at her age, although he'd certainly never realized she had such a passion for travel! He did wish her well, but the thought of having two strangers living with him indefinitely was disturbing. Especially when one of the strangers was a beautiful redhead, and the other a two-year-old elf!

And yet . . . He remembered how he'd felt earlier this evening, coming home after working late again, driving through his front gate, seeing his house with all its lights on, every window bright and welcoming.

And then he'd walked into the silence. She's upstairs probably putting Wendy to bed, he'd told himself, denying feelings of disappointment. He'd gone into the kitchen and found the sandwich on the counter, covered with a cloth napkin. The note had been propped up in front of it.

"I hope you like tuna, it was all I could find. I'll go shopping tomorrow. If there's anything you need, please leave me a list." It was signed with an *E*. And then, *"P.S. Wendy and I are in the last two rooms on the west side, if that's okay with you."*

He'd eaten the sandwich standing at the counter, and then had gone straight up to his office, taking the note with him. At the top of the stairs he'd paused for a moment, unable to keep his gaze from going to the far end of the hall, where two open doorways spilled twin rectangles of light onto the carpet. He could hear voices, one low-pitched, husky, unintelligible, the other higher and less restrained. He heard a child's giggle, and then softly, singing. He even recognized the song, "Puff, the Magic Dragon." He'd stood there for a few minutes, frowning, wondering if he ought to go and say something, announce himself, say hello . . . or good night. *Hi, honey, I'm home.*

Instead, he'd gone to the attic feeling like an intruder in his own house. He'd turned on the word processor, but instead of tuning in on the travails of Princess Kerissa, he'd plugged in a fresh disk, typed the words, *SHOPPING LIST*, and centered them on the monitor screen. Under that, after half an hour of intense concentration, he'd written, *cat food*. His mother's phone call had not been an unwelcome interruption.

Now, thinking of Wendy, he added *milk* to the list. And then erased it. Elizabeth would take care of her child's needs without any reminders from him!

He sat back in his chair, frowning. The house was very quiet. Which was, of course, exactly the way Culley liked—no, *needed* it to be.

Dammit, it was *too* quiet.

Resigned to the fact that he wasn't going to get anything of value accomplished tonight, Culley turned off the computer, locked his office, and went back down the attic stairs. At his bedroom door, he paused. The far end of the hallway was dark and silent; all the doors were closed.

His own door had been left ajar for the cat; he pushed it open the rest of the way and walked in. Moving silently, following established routines, he began to undress for bed. He saw no need to turn on a light. The moon and stars and city lights provided adequate illumination, and besides, he knew his way around the room blindfolded. Glasses, watch, and the contents of his pockets went on the dresser top, shoes on the floor in the closet. Slacks, shirt, and underwear on the chair. He was about to cross the hall to the bathroom naked, as he always did, but remembered just in time that things were different now. He wasn't alone in the house. Muttering to himself, he went back for a robe.

Wearing the short black silk kimono Shannon had bought for him in Maui on their honeymoon, Culley left his bedroom, strode across the hall, opened the bathroom door and walked in.

A small, shocked gasp stopped him in his tracks.

Four

At precisely the same moment, two voices with almost the same quality of breathlessness said, "Oh God, I'm sorry."

They'd met in the doorway. Elizabeth had obviously just been leaving; she'd already turned off the light. Steam and fragrance wafted from the interior of the bathroom, evoking sensory memories of tropical nights, flower gardens, and summer rains, wrapping them in warmth and intimacy as palpable as a shared blanket.

"I was—I didn't think you'd be . . ." Elizabeth sagged against the doorframe. In the semidarkness Culley heard the soft sigh of her escaping breath. "I'm really sorry."

She was wearing a towel turban and a dark-colored bathrobe. From the delicate oval of her face to the deep slash in the front of the robe, her skin had its own luminescence, like alabaster in moonlight.

"It's okay," Culley croaked, watching the shadows of her lashes settle like feathers onto her cheeks.

"No. I should have asked. But . . . the showerhead in the other bathroom seems to be broken, and since you were working, I didn't want to bother you."

"It's quite all right," Culley said, and cleared his throat, knowing he sounded as stiff and gruff as a Victorian papa. All he could think about was the way the sultry heat of her body was penetrating the thin fabric of his kimono, touching him like an all-over caress.

"I'd better go." It was almost a gasp.

"Yes. All right." His throat felt like a gravel road.

Her voice drifted back to him as she slipped like a wraith through the door. "Good night."

"Good night," Culley said to the empty darkness, aware only then that his heart was beating hard and fast.

Close Encounters of the Unthinkable Kind, he warned himself as he turned on the lights and the shower. But think about it he did, just the same. His mind was a stew, a swamp, a kaleidoscope of images, some of which were half-forgotten memories, some newborn fantasies . . . all impossible. He scolded himself. Elizabeth was his housekeeper, his employee. She was living under his roof, and therefore, under his protection. And for her to him moved in with him so readily, Culley realized, his mother must have told her he could be trusted to behave honorably and responsibly. It came to him as a double take: She trusted him.

And, he thought, if Elizabeth and his mother could read his mind, Elizabeth would be packing her bags, and his mother would be on the next plane back to Los Angeles!

He'd just have to be more careful, he told himself, to avoid any more confrontations. First thing tomorrow he'd see about fixing that showerhead, so at least they wouldn't be stumbling over each other in the bathroom. It was going to be tough enough having a beautiful, desirable woman around all the time. If he had to shave with her lingering fragrance permeating his pores, he'd probably cut his own throat.

Back in his room he turned on the light so he

could write himself a note about the showerhead. He was rummaging through the odds and ends on his dresser top, looking for a pen and something to write on, when he heard a slight rustling noise . . . a faint sigh. He turned, looked, and froze.

He was still standing there a moment later when Elizabeth burst into his room without knocking, looking pale and panic-stricken, her hair tumbling over her shoulders in wild wet curls. "I can't find Wendy!" she gasped. "She's not—oh . . ."

Momentum had carried her to Culley's side. They stood together, looking at his bed and at the little girl who lay asleep in the middle of it.

She was wearing pajamas, the kind with feet in them. They were yellow, almost the same shade as the hair that poured like spilled sunshine across the dark bedspread. Rosebud mouth softly snoring . . . cheeks sleep-flushed . . . arms flung wide, hands curled like flower petals . . . She was a vision of innocence, a watercolor in pink and gold except for the tiny black and white kitten that lay across her neck, nestled just beneath her chin. And Culley thought he'd never in his life seen anything so beautiful.

And then he looked down at Elizabeth. The expression on her face stopped his breathing. He actually felt it catch in his chest with a painful bump, and for a moment or two he couldn't speak.

Elizabeth sighed.

Culley said gruffly, "This is getting to be a habit."

"She wanted to say good night to the kitties. I told her no, because—" Her eyes, which had lifted beseechingly to his face, suddenly dropped to the front of his kimono. Reflexively, Culley's hand went to the place that had drawn her attention—and encountered bare chest. He watched the movement of her throat as she swallowed.

He muttered, "It's all right," just as she said, "I'm

so sorry." It seemed to him that the temperature in the room had risen sharply.

She was moving away from him, speaking rapidly in a low voice. "Dr. Ward, it won't happen again, I promise. I promise, I'll see that Wendy doesn't—"

Culley caught her by the arm and turned her to face him. Her eyes flicked to his face—startled eyes, the soft gray of rain-drenched skies. He saw the telltale smudges of exhaustion beneath them, and the slight trembling of her lips, and felt a heaviness in his chest he knew was pity . . . and a similar heaviness farther down he knew was not.

"I see my mother's told you all about me," he said softly.

Tiny lines of confusion appeared around her eyes, though they continued to cling to his as if to a lifeline. "What do you mean?"

"I guess she told you that I'm the neighborhood Dr. Frankenstein, right?" He sighed. "Damn. There goes my cover."

Her lips, unsure whether to smile or not, compromised by parting slightly. Culley put his hands on her shoulders, resisting the urge to rub and caress the contours of muscle and bone beneath the fabric of her robe.

"The attic room where I conduct all sorts of evil and grotesque experiments . . . and the fact that I keep unwary guests locked up in the basement and use them for spare body parts? She must have told you about those too."

A breathy giggle escaped her. "She did not."

"No?" And then, very gently, "Then how come you think I'm some kind of monster?"

She caught her lower lip between her teeth, and a tiny frown appeared between her eyes. "I don't think you're a monster. But . . ." Her gaze dropped once more to the front of his robe. He decided it would be all right if he tightened his hands, a little, on her shoulders, just a gentle, reassuring squeeze. "But you're my employer," she finished, stating it with flat simplicity.

"Yes." Culley let his hands slide away from her shoulders as she turned back toward the bed. And then, intercepting her, "Here, I'll get her." Gently, carefully, he took the newborn kitten from its nesting place and handed it to Elizabeth, then gathered the sleeping child into his arms. Wendy sighed, muttered indistinctly, and settled against his chest. "Where do you want her?" he whispered, stirring wisps of silken hair with his breath.

"This way." After one quick, uncertain look, she slipped ahead of him through the door. As he followed her down the hallway, he noticed the way she moved in her bare feet and dark blue bathrobe—her walk self-conscious, not sexy at all. And yet he knew he'd never forget it, the way she looked at just that moment.

In the bedroom she'd chosen for Wendy, Elizabeth smoothed the rumpled bed and folded back the covers, then stood aside. As gently and carefully as he knew how, Culley laid the sleeping child down. She immediately rolled over onto her tummy, and made chuckling sounds when he pulled the blankets up and tucked them around her.

Not knowing what else to do then, feeling awkward and extraneous, he moved away. When he looked back, he saw Elizabeth bending over her daughter, holding her hair out of the way with one hand, her face soft with tenderness and maternal concern. In the moonlight there were no colors, just shades of gray and indigo. It seemed to Culley like a black and white photograph, stark in its beauty, all the more emotionally affecting for being without the distractions of color.

Emotions he couldn't name made Culley turn silently away.

• • •

On her third day in the house, Elizabeth discovered the library. It was near the back of the house, off the living room, behind a door she had assumed to be a closet. In a more modern house, she supposed, it would be called a den, and she ventured into it timidly, at first, as into some private sanctum. But Dr. Ward—*Culley*—hadn't said anything about its being forbidden territory, unlike that office of his in the attic, which he had told her was strictly off-limits, and which he kept locked all the time anyway, so that she couldn't even dust or vacuum in there.

Though dim and dusty, the room had a lived-in look about it, a certain friendly untidiness that seemed to be due more to the eclectic nature of the well-thumbed books themselves, rather than any real clutter. No elegant, leather-bound volumes, these, purchased with an eye for color and design rather than content. These books had been read, many of them over and over again.

It gave Elizabeth a little thrill of excitement to move along the bookcases, trailing her fingers over tattered jackets and creased spines, tilting her head sideways in order to read titles. So these were Dr. Ward's books. . . . A great reader herself, Elizabeth felt she could learn a lot about a person by the books he enjoyed.

She had to admit to a growing curiosity about her employer. She realized that she knew very little about him, except for what his mother had told her, which was that his wife had died of cancer very suddenly about five years ago, and that he'd become somewhat reclusive after her death. She knew that as a scientist, he'd been considered sort of a "boy wonder," but she didn't know what he did, exactly, and was sure she wouldn't understand it if she did. She knew that he didn't *look* like a scientist.

Elizabeth wasn't sure what she had expected, but she was pleasantly surprised by the contents of Dr.

Ward's library. She saw a lot of her old friends there—A. A. Milne and E. B. White, P. G. Wodehouse and Mark Twain, the murder mysteries of Rex Stout, Anne McCaffrey's dragon books—a strange mix, arranged in no particular order—Charles Schulz's "Peanuts" mixed in with the works of Shakespeare, Kipling, and the histories of Will and Ariel Durant. She found it reassuring that a man of Dr. Ward's intellect had, at some point in his life, enjoyed Snoopy and Winnie-the-Pooh.

It was odd, Elizabeth thought, how hard it had become to think of him as anything but "Dr. Ward." He seemed so aloof, so austere, so formidable.

It certainly hadn't been that way at first. How vividly she remembered his endearing helplessness over the kittens' birth, the strange intimacy of that night, and the touching way he'd covered her and Wendy and left them sleeping. She remembered the next morning, too, the nova of sheer delight that had burst inside her with the realization that the learned and distinguished scientist had actually slid down the banister! And then, of course, there had been that evening in the bathroom, when she had found herself facing him across a narrow doorway.

She remembered the way he'd looked then, with his hair in attractive disarray, his robe negligently knotted, its deep slash a shadowed reminder of the masculine mysteries underneath. She remembered the look in his eyes—not at all formidable, certainly not austere, anything but aloof! And most of all she remembered the way the look had made her *feel*, heavy and weak-kneed, as if his eyes were a great weight, pressing on her body.

She hadn't seen much of him since that night; he seemed to be deliberately trying to avoid her, which was probably just as well. As she'd said that night, he was her employer. He had given her this job, and a place for her and Wendy to live in his own house. Elizabeth knew he'd done so against his own inclination, and she was fairly certain he'd done so primarily because of his mother's recommendation. It came to her as a small shock to realize that they trusted her.

And, Elizabeth thought as she leaned weakly against a bookcase and pressed her hands to her hot cheeks, if they could read her mind at this moment, Dr. Ward would probably fire her on the spot, and Mrs. Ward would be on the first plane back to Los Angeles!

Resolutely pushing aside disturbing thoughts, Elizabeth plugged in the vacuum cleaner. It should be easier to keep such thoughts at bay from now on, she reflected as she snapped a long-handled dusting brush to the end of the hose, since the kittens' box had been moved to the kitchen and Culley could shut his bedroom door now. Wendy hadn't quite figured out how to manipulate the big old-fashioned doorknobs yet, thank goodness, but she had taken to crawling into her mother's bed in the middle of the night, a habit Elizabeth was determined to nip in the bud, once Wendy had had a chance to adjust to all the changes in her life.

And Elizabeth had made sure the bathroom wouldn't be a problem anymore. The very next day, she had picked up a new showerhead in the hardware department at the supermarket, and had installed it with the help of some tools she'd found in the garage.

A glance at her watch told her that she still had a good half hour before Wendy would be waking up from her nap, so she pressed the vacuum cleaner's ON switch with her toe, reached behind her to turn on the Walkman she'd tucked into her hip pocket, and adjusted the earphones over her head. A moment later she was enthusiastically attacking the cobwebs above the bookcases to the exultant beat of "Proud Mary."

• • •

Wendy was having a dream about kitties. Kitties—not little squirmy sausage-kitties, but fat, fluffy, roly-poly kitties, like the ones she'd seen on TV—were falling from the sky like snowflakes. She was laughing and running around, trying to catch one before they fell to the ground and ran away from her. Finally the daddy came and lifted her up onto his shoulders. And then he reached out with his big hand and plucked a kitty from the air and put it right into her arms. She laughed and hugged it tightly, and it meowed very loudly and woke her up.

She sat up in bed and rubbed her eyes. A great big black kitty was sitting on the floor of her bed, blinking at her. When Wendy said, "Hi, kitty," he meowed and jumped off the bed. Wendy scrambled down off the bed too, dragging the covers with her, but when she tried to pick up the big kitty, he slipped away from her and ran out of the room. Wendy said, "Uh oh, come back, kitty," and ran after him.

The big black kitty ran down the hall and up the steep stairs, the ones Mommy had told her not to climb. But Wendy wasn't thinking about Mommy, she just wanted to pet the big black kitty.

When the kitty saw Wendy coming up the stairs, he put his ears back and disappeared through a little door, one of the ones Mommy had told Wendy not to crawl through. Wendy did think about Mommy this time. She hesitated, then put her head through the little door and called, as sweetly as she knew how, "Come on, nice kitty, come on."

And then Wendy saw something that made her forget all about Mommy *and* the big black kitty. She crowed, "Toys!" and slipped through the little door.

Elizabeth was sitting cross-legged on the floor beside the silent vacuum cleaner, with the headphones around her neck, sniffling over Frances Hodgson Burnett's "The Secret Garden." When the mantel clock in the living room began to strike, she gave a guilty start and looked at her watch.

Good heavens, she thought, four o'clock! Wendy never slept that late. She should have been up long ago.

She scrambled to her feet, dumping the book and the Walkman onto the rug beside the vacuum cleaner, and almost ran to the stairs. It's all right, she told herself, but being a mother's, her heart wasn't listening. It knew.

The house was very quiet. Too quiet. Elizabeth's footsteps were thunderous in the upstairs hallway. The door to Wendy's room stood open; bursting through it, she found her fears realized. The bed was empty, its covers rumpled and trailing onto the floor. It's all right, she told herself, she's just hiding. Wendy's favorite game at the moment was hide-and-seek.

She called, "Wendy?" as she looked under the bed, in the closet, behind the curtains. "Where are you, baby? Come out now."

She went into her own room and did the same thing, and then stood still with her hands clasped to her forehead, trying not to panic. Where could she have gone? All the other doors along the hall were closed.

Downstairs. Downstairs, she knew, there must be a hundred places where a child could hide. Oh dear God, she wouldn't go outside, would she? She couldn't manage the doorknobs, but what about the kitty doors?

With her heart hammering so hard she could barely breathe, Elizabeth almost vaulted down the stairs. Halfway down, she thought she heard a noise and paused with her hand on the banister to listen. It came again. She called, "Wendy?" trying to hold her breath, trying to still the thunder of her heartbeat.

The reply came faintly, and impossibly, from overhead. "Mommy, I'm in *here!*"

Elizabeth whispered "Oh, thank God," and sagged for a moment against the banister. "Wendy, where are you, honey?"

"In here!"

Where? "Wendy, I can't see you. Can you tell me where you are?" Ears straining, she started slowly back up the stairs.

"I climbed up the stairs," Wendy said, sounding pleased with herself. That was followed by some unintelligible babble, of which Elizabeth could make out only the word *kitty.*

But by this time she was standing at the foot of the attic stairs and was staring up them in disbelief and dread. "Wendy, are you up there?" Please, God, she couldn't be.

"Yep," Wendy confirmed happily, "up *here.*"

Oh God, she was in Dr. Ward's private office. How could she have gotten in? Elizabeth wondered. Unless he'd forgotten to lock the door—no, it was locked, all right. What now?

"Wendy, what are you *doing* in there?"

"I'm playin' with toys."

Toys? What in the world would a nuclear physicist have in his office that a two-year-old might consider toys? The possibilities were nightmarish.

Sinking onto the top of the staircase, Elizabeth leaned her head against the door and closed her eyes. "Oh Wendy, honey, how did you get in there?"

The reply was another stream of gibberish, of which Elizabeth again made out only the word *kitty.* And suddenly she understood. *The kitty door.* It was right there at her elbow. Wendy had crawled through the kitty door!

"Wendy," she cooed to the door panels in her most patient, winning tone, "it's time to come out now. It's almost dinnertime. Can you crawl out through the little door?"

"No," Wendy said reasonably, "I'm playin' with toys."

Elizabeth uttered a word under her breath that

she wouldn't have wanted to become a part of her daughter's vocabulary. "What kind of toys are you playing with, baby?"

There was a thoughtful pause, and then, decisively, "Puppets."

Puppets? "Wendy," Elizabeth said, pushing honey-eyed tones through gritted teeth, "put the puppets away, now, okay? It's time to come out."

"I'm *playin'*."

Elizabeth groaned in sheer frustration; she recognized that tone of voice. Abandoning diplomacy, she banged on the door with her fist and shouted, "Wendy, you come out of there *right now*, do you hear me? I mean it!"

No answer.

Elizabeth looked at her watch. Four-thirty. Culley could be home as early as five. Then again, he might not be home until ten or eleven. And here she sat, completely at the mercy of an obstinate, mule-headed two-year-old, who at this very moment could be *playing* with some sort of nuclear time bomb! Culley must have had a good reason for keeping that room locked and off-limits.

She had to get Wendy out of there.

But how? Break the door down? Better yet, call the fire department and let *them* break the door down.

The thought of Dr. Ward coming home from work to find his front yard full of fire trucks, his house full of strangers in yellow slickers, and his private office full of splinters, was a chilling one indeed. There had to be a better way, Elizabeth thought. A quieter way.

It came to her suddenly, a memory of something heard or read long ago and filed away for just this occasion: Take the door off its hinges. Yes! It could be done; the hinges were on this side of the door. She didn't even need the fire department. It was something she could do, with the tools she'd found in the garage!

With a breathless, "Wendy, don't go away, I'll be right back!" Elizabeth hurled herself down the stairs. Fifteen minutes and several bruised knuckles later, she was easing the door off its hinges and sliding it carefully to one side. A moment more, and she was stepping into Culley's private office, feeling a lot like Eve must have felt when she reached for the forbidden fruit.

"Hi, Mommy!" Wendy had no such qualms. She was delighted to have company.

But Elizabeth was too stunned to answer her. Whatever she might have expected to find, even in her wildest imaginings, it could never have prepared her for this.

As Culley was coming up the driveway he thought he saw a light in the attic window. He told himself it was impossible. He *knew* he'd locked the door when he'd finished last night, and besides, Elizabeth would never . . .

When he looked again it was gone, and he told himself it had just been a reflection or his imagination.

He came through his front door, bracing himself for the greeting he was coming to expect: A flurry of footsteps, a joyous shout, "Hi, Daddy!" and a pair of small arms wrapped around his leg. When he was met instead by silence, he gave a soft, rueful chuckle and shook his head. Amazing, he thought, how quickly he'd gotten used to that.

Well, he was home earlier than usual, he told himself as he poked his head into the downstairs rooms, trying not to admit that he was looking for anyone. The shipment of xenon he'd been expecting hadn't arrived, and since it was Friday anyway, he'd decided to call it a day. He was thinking of taking the weekend off, too, from his word processor as well as the lab. Maybe he'd even go somewhere. He caught himself wondering whether Elizabeth would enjoy the Huntington Library . . . though he thought Wendy would probably prefer the zoo.

When he saw the library door open he knew Elizabeth had been there. He smiled when he saw the book and the tape player on the floor beside the vacuum cleaner, and picking up the Walkman, casually pressed the ON button. It gave him a little bit of a shock to hear Creedence Clearwater Revival coming from the headset. Funny, he'd have thought CCR a little before Elizabeth's time.

Outside in the hall again, he heard the bump of footsteps on the stairs. At the sound, his heart gave a little bump of its own, and he went to stand at the foot of the staircase to wait for them to descend.

In old jeans and a sweatshirt several sizes too big for her, Elizabeth looked like a prepubescent tomboy just in from climbing trees. Her hair was caught back in a ponytail, and there was a smudge of something across one flushed cheek. In one hand she was carrying his dad's old wooden tool caddy; the other had a firm grip on Wendy's arm. Wendy didn't look happy.

"Everything okay?" Culley asked casually, leaning against the newel post.

Elizabeth gave him a dazzling smile. "Oh sure, yeah, everything's just fine."

Culley nodded toward the toolbox. "Something else malfunctioning? Why don't you call a plumber?"

"What? Oh, no, it wasn't anything like that. See, it was . . . I was just . . . it was a door. Some hinges needed tightening." She took a deep breath and shrugged her shoulders, smiling. "Nothing important. All taken care of."

"Want *toys*," Wendy said grumpily, digging a fist into her eye.

Culley glanced at her, then raised an eyebrow at her mother.

"I'm afraid Wendy's not very happy with me." Elizabeth sounded breathless, and her cheeks seemed to have grown pinker. "She didn't want to put the toys away when I told her it was dinnertime. Speaking of which—"

"Want *puppets!*"

"—I'm sorry dinner's not ready. I must have lost track of time. It'll only take—"

"It's all right, I'm early," Culley murmured as she hurried past him, towing an uncooperative Wendy. "Take your time." He started up the stairs, then changed his mind and followed Elizabeth into the kitchen.

She was at the sink, holding Wendy like a sack under one arm while she washed the little girl's face and hands under the running faucet. When she heard the kitchen door bang, she started nervously and said over her shoulder, "Oh, can I get you something? A drink, or . . .?"

Culley thought she looked remarkably pretty, all flushed and rumpled, with tendrils of hair escaping from the ponytail and curling around her face and neck. He felt a disturbing desire to go closer to her.

Instead, he said, "Thanks, I'll do it," crossed to the refrigerator, took out the orange juice and set it down on the table. The cupboard with glasses in it was on the other side of the sink. Elizabeth gave him a quick look and reached for it, just as he murmured, "No, no, I'll get it," and put a restraining hand on her shoulder.

Muscle, bone and sinew . . . what was there in that to make his own flesh heat and tingle so that he couldn't seem to keep his fingers from rubbing back and forth over the fabric of her sweatshirt?

He heard the slight break in her breathing as her eyes met his over the top of her daughter's head. For a moment she froze, her mouth slightly open, her head at a quizzical tilt, as if she were hearing sounds she couldn't identify. And then action resumed, as if someone had pushed the START button: Her mouth snapped shut, her lashes dropped. Culley lifted his hand from her shoulder; she leaned over to place Wendy on the floor. Culley leaned over to take a glass from the cupboard. She became very busy drying Wendy's hands and face with a dishtowel; he poured orange juice into the glass with meticulous care.

Running out of things to do, they both ventured at the same moment to break the silence.

"About this weekend—"

"I've been meaning to ask—"

"You go first," Culley said, sitting down at the table with his glass of juice.

"I want *juice!*"

Elizabeth sighed. "What do you say, Wendy?"

"*Please!*"

"I was just wondering about this weekend," Elizabeth said as she complied with her daughter's request. "Um . . . we didn't exactly talk about, you know . . . days off and things like that."

Aha! Culley thought, mentally snapping his fingers; he'd known there were questions he should have been asking!

"Or about your salary," he said, frowning at his orange juice. "I'm really sorry. Do you need money? And by any chance, did my mother happen to mention how much I'm paying you?"

She was making impatient motions with her hand. "No, no, that's all right. She told me how much the job paid, and I said that would be fine. But about this week—"

"Would you mind telling *me* how much I'm paying you?"

She did. "Good Lord, is that all?" Culley asked, a little shocked.

Her dimple appeared, and he realized with a strange pang that he hadn't seen it since that first night, not since she'd come to work for him, in fact. "Well, I suppose you could give me a raise." And then, before he could respond to that, she laughed and made erasing motions again with her hands. "No, it's really very fair. Don't forget, you're also giving both Wendy and me room and board. No, what I wanted to talk to you about was whether you wanted me to work weekends, and take my days off during the week, or whether I should take weekends off. Of course, if there's anything special you need me for, I'll always be glad . . ."

Her days off. Of course. He hadn't even been considering the fact that she'd want time for herself. He didn't own her; she wasn't his wife, she was his employee. Of course she had her own life, friends, family. Places to go, people to see.

The thought left him feeling inexplicably depressed.

"Whatever works out best for you," he said neutrally, drinking the last of his orange juice. "Just let me know."

"Well, in that case, since tomorrow's Saturday, is it okay if I—"

"Fine. That's fine." He got up to put his glass in the sink, and then, since it seemed to make her nervous to have him staying in the kitchen, he went upstairs to work until dinnertime.

As he was leaving he heard Wendy say, "Where's Daddy goin', Mom?" The door closed before he could hear her mother's reply.

It was just as well, he said to himself while he waited for his computer to warm up; he was behind schedule anyway. He really did need to work, and he'd get a lot more accomplished this weekend without the distraction of strangers in the house.

The small green characters on the computer screen blurred and ran together, and Culley saw instead a pair of gray-green eyes, the look in them neither startled nor surprised, but intent, as if there were a hundred questions they wanted to ask. By closing his own eyes he could recall the shape of her mouth, the way her lips looked, breathlessly parted, the nervous movements of her tongue, and of her throat when she swallowed. If he inhaled deeply, he could almost smell that lemony fragrance of her hair mingled with the clean, warm scent of her body, uniquely feminine, uniquely *hers*.

And suddenly he found that he was rubbing his hand back and forth on his thigh, as if by doing so he could scrub away the imprint of Elizabeth's shoulder from the palm of his hand. But that subtle friction only sensitized his nerve endings, awakened his responses, stirred up sensual memories, making it impossible for him to deny any longer that what he'd wanted to do more than anything else in the world, at that moment, was turn his housekeeper into his arms and kiss her.

Five

"Don't want to go shoppin'!" Wendy resisted Elizabeth's efforts to corral her silky hair into a ponytail. "Don't want rubber band!" She tore the ponytail holder out of her hair and hurled it to the floor.

"Oh, Wendy." Elizabeth sighed, sinking down onto the bed with the brush in her lap. The truth was, she didn't want to go shopping either.

Sunshine and birdsong called her to the window. Raising it all the way, she inhaled cool morning air that smelled of cut grass and moist earth, nameless flowers and dead brown leaves, with a hint of wood smoke and city smog. It was Sunday, another gorgeous autumn morning, too beautiful to spend indoors. It was, in fact, another day like yesterday, a day Elizabeth had spent tramping up and down the shopping mall, pushing Wendy's stroller, dodging hordes of teenagers and other strollers, killing time until she could take Wendy home and put her down for her nap. After nap time, she'd taken Wendy to a park she'd spotted near the mall and let her play on the swings until dusk, which came much too early in November. They'd had supper at McDonald's, dragging it out as long as possible, and then had stopped for ice cream cones on the way home, but that had still left nearly two hours before she could reasonably expect Wendy to be ready to go back to bed. She'd managed to fill the time with crayons and books and a bath, but the fact was, the weekend was only half over—her *first* weekend—and she was already running out of ideas for keeping Wendy out of Dr. Ward's hair!

"What doin', Mom? Wanna see too!" Wendy was trying to chin herself on the windowsill.

"Oh, baby," Elizabeth sighed, lifting her into her arms, "what am I going to do with you?"

When she'd promised Culley that Wendy wouldn't disturb his work, she hadn't been thinking about weekends! And now that Wendy had discovered the wonders behind that locked door . . . why, it was so incredible that Elizabeth was still having trouble believing it herself.

"I see it!" Wendy cried joyfully, pointing at something in the brilliant autumn sky that only she could see. And then, bouncing and patting her mother's face—not gently—with both hands, "Want to go outside!"

And why not? Elizabeth thought, hugging her squirming, giggling daughter. They hadn't really had a chance to explore their new home yet. They could spend the day right here, but outdoors. She'd pack a lunch—a picnic! Dr. Ward wouldn't even know they were around.

He came into the kitchen while Elizabeth was putting together the picnic lunch. She hadn't heard his step on the stairs, so there wasn't time to prepare herself. When the door opened and Wendy sang out, "Hi, Daddy!" she started and dropped a jelly-smeared slice of bread on the floor—jelly side down, of course. She dove after it, glad for the excuse to hide her face from him a moment longer.

She told herself that the lurching sensation she felt under her ribs, as if she'd been socked in the stomach, must be guilt. After all, she'd violated his sanctum and discovered his incredible secret. She told herself she really was going to have to get ahold of herself and stop blushing and stammering every time she saw him, or he was going to start getting suspicious. A man as brilliant as Dr. Ward would probably put two and two together sooner or later!

As she was dabbing ineffectually at the jelly smears with a dry washcloth, she heard him say, "Hi, squirt, what are you doing?" Not to her—Wendy was sitting cross-legged on the kitchen table, slapping peanut butter onto a piece of bread with more industry than accuracy.

"I'm makin' a samwich," Wendy announced happily. "Want some?" When Culley laughingly declined, she offered the peanut buttery knife instead to Prissy, who had just jumped up on the table to investigate, leaving her kittens mewing piteously in their box.

With nervous tremors cascading through her body, Elizabeth watched Culley's feet come around the table and stop just beyond the mess on the floor. She noticed that there were holes in the toes of his tennis shoes. She found it oddly touching.

"That's one of the basic laws of physics, you know," he said gravely, his voice drifting down to her like a warm and gentle rain. "The bread always lands jelly side down."

He squatted down in front of her, balancing on the balls of his feet. He was wearing jeans so old and supple they'd acquired the matte velvet softness of skin, and a blue chambray work shirt with the sleeves rolled to just below the elbows. She noticed that there were drops of moisture in the indentation at the base of his throat and the beginnings of stubble on his chin. Beyond that, her eyes refused to go.

She mumbled, "Really?" and went on dabbing at the jelly. Her hands felt jerky and uncoordinated.

"Scientific fact." He stood up, dusted his hands and picked up a carrot stick from the counter. "Is this breakfast or lunch?"

Elizabeth rose, dumped the bread and washcloth into the sink and glanced distractedly at Wendy, who was licking peanut butter off one set of fingers while Prissy worked on the other. "It's lunch, I guess. A picnic, actually."

"Picnic!" Wendy confirmed, beaming messily.

"Oh yeah?" Culley raised his eyebrows in an interested way and bit into the carrot stick. "Where are you planning to go?"

Elizabeth waved her hand, then noticed the jelly on it and wiped it on her thigh. "Oh, nowhere, really. Just outside—you know, in the yard. We thought we'd kind of explore. That is, if it's all right with you. We don't want to disturb—"

"Would you like a guide?"

Elizabeth's heart stopped beating for a second or two, then resumed with a new and wilder rhythm.

"I think I'd be a good one," Culley said with a casual shrug. "At least I'm familiar with the territory."

"Are you—do you mean you want to come with us?"

"Sure. If it's all right. I mean, I wouldn't want to interfere with your plans."

"No! No. I'd love to have you. Wendy—"

"How about it, squirt?" Culley touched the end of Wendy's peanut butter-smeared nose, making her giggle. "Is it okay if I come with you on your picnic?"

Wendy's nod made her whole body bounce. "Yeah!" And then, just in case her mother had missed it, "Daddy's comin' . . . picnic, Mom!"

"Have you got enough food for three?" Culley asked, smiling.

The smile was for Elizabeth. It warmed her all over, made her feel tingly and alive, full of life and promise, like newly turned earth touched by spring sunshine. It had been so long since she'd felt like that, she had trouble recognizing it for what it was at first. *Happiness.* Pure happiness.

"Plenty, if you like peanut butter," she said, pulling in a shaky breath and smiling back.

Culley showed his teeth and said through them, "*Love* it."

Elizabeth released her breath in a gust of laughter and handed him a knife. "Great! In that case, here—you can cut up those apples and put them in a plastic bag."

"I can manage that, I think. And then what?"

"Let's see . . . put them in Wendy's lunch box. I guess it's on the table."

Culley picked it up and raised a quizzical eyebrow. "Solar the Antarian? What's with this kid, anyway?"

Wendy snatched the lunch box and clutched it jealously to her chest. "*My toys!*"

A bubble of laughter and wonder inside Elizabeth grew and swelled until it made her want to dance and burst into song. She managed only a shrug and a serene little smile. "Strange, isn't it? I guess there's just no accounting for taste."

"Hmm . . . best peanut butter and jelly sandwich I ever ate," Culley said with a replete sigh, as he stretched himself out on his side and propped his head on one hand.

They had picnicked in the grape arbor behind the gardener's shed in the calico light of November sunshine filtered through golden leaves. Now Culley was lying on the blanket, while Elizabeth sat in an old wooden swing, lazily rocking, lulled by its slow, rhythmic creaking. Wendy had enjoyed the creaky swing, too, but had left it for a new game Culley called the raisin solution.

"Sheer genius," Elizabeth had said in a whispered aside, as Wendy busily gathered the last withered grapes the birds had missed and put them into her Solar the Antarian thermos bottle.

"Sheer desperation," Culley had replied.

"It's probably the wine coolers," she said now, giving the swing another push with her toe. Wendy was totally engrossed in the raisin game, leaving Elizabeth free to notice again the way Culley's hair hung over his forehead and brushed the collar of his shirt. She was changing her mind about him needing a haircut, though. She decided she liked his hair long. It looked as if it would be nice to touch.

"I found them in the refrigerator," she said, drawing another of those uneven breaths. "I hope it was all right."

"Not mine. Probably left over from one of my mother's bridge parties," Culley muttered, and added with a dry chuckle, "Somehow I don't think she's going to miss 'em in Tahiti."

"Tahiti? I thought she was going to Mexico."

He gave a one-shouldered shrug. "I guess I forgot to tell you. I had a call from her. Seems she'd decided to go on to Tahiti after the Mexico cruise."

"I see," Elizabeth said carefully, watching her toe make designs in the dirt beneath the swing.

Culley was making designs on the blanket with the bottom of the wine bottle. "I guess I'll be needing you a little longer than originally planned. Unless . . . is that going to be a problem for you?"

"Oh no," Elizabeth murmured, "it's no problem."

"Good. Good."

There was silence, filled with the creaking of the swing, the hum of insects, the distant drone of an airplane . . . and the loud, heavy thud of her heartbeat. She wanted to jump up and shout and hug someone, but instead, after a while she said lightly, looking up into the leafy canopy, "This is a nice place for a picnic. So quiet, peaceful."

"Yeah." Culley's voice sounded sleepy. "I've always like it. Do you know that the first time I ever kissed a girl was right here. I think I was eleven."

"Oh really? Let me guess. Were her initials S. H.?"

"No. Her name was Amy Weismuller. She lived next door. Why do you ask?"

His voice was still soft, but it seemed to have gone flat. Elizabeth glanced over at him and shrugged. "I just wondered. Those are the initials that are carved on this swing." She traced the rough grooves with her fingertips. "S. H., see?"

Culley took his glasses off and began, with great concentration, to wipe them on his shirttail. After a moment he cleared his throat and said in a neutral voice, "That's my wife. Her name was Shannon."

"Oh," Elizabeth said. The stab of pain surprised her, but she didn't back away from it, or from the subject. "Shannon?"

"Just Shannon. Oh, her maiden name was Wilder, but when she carved that it was already Ward. We'd been married . . . oh, maybe a month, when I first brought her here." He gave a soft laugh as he put his glasses on, then leaned back on his hands. "I remember the day she did that," he said, nodding at the carving. "Those aren't initials. She was going to carve her whole name, only she—we got sidetracked, I guess."

He was silent for a few moments, remembering. Elizabeth watched his throat move in a small, painful convulsion, and felt her own throat tighten in empathy . . . and something else. In a strange way, she envied him. At least, she thought, most of his memories were happy ones.

"She used to like to say her whole name," Culley went on, smiling now, speaking easily of good times. "Shannon Wilder Ward. She liked to say she definitely was the *Wilder* Ward. God, she had so much energy! Did you know she was an athlete?" Elizabeth shook her head. "Tennis. A pro. When I met her I think she was seeded tenth at Wimbledon. And she was on her way up too. After we were married I encouraged her to keep on with it, but all she really wanted to do was . . ." His voice trailed off and he looked away. Elizabeth saw a little muscle move in his jaw.

"What?" she prompted huskily, unable to bear not knowing.

Culley coughed and raked a hand through his hair. "She wanted kids . . . we both did. She couldn't wait to start a family. That's why we moved back here, to this house. Dad had just retired, and he and Mom had their eye on a condo in Laguna. So I bought the house from them. It's a good house for kids." He was silent for a moment, then drew a deep breath. "I was an only child and so was she."

"I was an only child too," Elizabeth said softly. "So I understand. I wouldn't want Wendy to be—" Her feet hit the ground, stopping the swing with a jolt. "Oh, God—speaking of Wendy, where *is* she?"

She and Culley were alone in the grape arbor.

Wendy was making raisin pies. She'd picked all the raisins she could reach and put them in her thermos, and added a couple handfuls of nice soft dirt and a few leaves and twigs for flavoring. What she needed now was water to make it nice and soupy.

Mommy and the daddy were talking, but that was okay; she didn't need to bother them, because she knew where there was some water. Lots of water. It was the place where the frogs lived, where the funny round leaves floated on top of the water. She'd wanted to stay there and play, but Mommy had said no, it wasn't a good place for a picnic, because there were too many bugs. But Wendy knew where the frog place was. She could find it all by herself.

"She can't go *too* far," Culley said. "The gate's closed." He glanced at Elizabeth and she turned to meet his gaze for a moment. He saw the fear in them, and in a flash of insight thought, It must be terrible to be a parent.

She gave a dry little laugh. "You don't know Wendy. You'd be amazed at what she can find to get into, the independent little stinker! *Darn* her! She was being so quiet, playing with those grapes. Where could she have gone?"

Culley put his hand on her arm. "Let's stop a minute . . . think. Where *would* she go? You know your daughter."

Elizabeth put a hand on her forehead and closed her eyes. "Okay, let's see. She likes to hide. She loves animals. What else?"

"She took the thermos with her, if that means anything."

"Okay, well, she had all those grapes in it, maybe she went to do something with them. Put them someplace. Oh damn . . . I don't know!" She called again, "*Wendy!* where are you?" They both listened to the silence.

After a moment Culley said slowly, as if he were unraveling a weighty scientific problem, "Consider this. She took the thermos. What does one put in a thermos?"

"Liquid," Elizabeth murmured, her eyes widening with the beginnings of inspiration. "Something to drink." Her voice escalated. "Maybe she was thirsty. Maybe she went to find some water."

"A faucet?" Culley ventured, but another thought was forming, one he didn't want to voice.

Elizabeth shook her head. "No, no, I don't think she'd know—oh God!" Her hands clutched at his forearms, and he knew that the same thought had just hit her. "The lily pond!" For one more anguished moment her eyes clung to his, and then he and Elizabeth turned together and sprinted for the front of the house.

"She wanted to stay there, remember," Elizabeth panted as they ran. "She wanted to play with the stupid frogs."

"It isn't deep," Culley muttered, trying to reassure himself as much as her. "It isn't deep. . . ."

The lily pond had been Shannon's idea. The original fountain had been damaged during the Sylmar quake and hadn't worked for years. When he and Shannon moved into the house, he was going to get rid of it, but she had suggested putting in water lilies instead. "It'll be fun," she'd said with that infectious enthusiasm of hers. "We'll get some goldfish, maybe some ducks." "Darling, I think ducks eat lilies," Culley had replied, indulgently. They'd settled for goldfish, but the last of them had died years ago.

They heard the baby crying as they reached the corner of the house. It was welcome music. The unthinkable dread banished, they looked at each other and ran even faster, their footsteps crunching in unison on the gravel drive, their breathing a ragged duet.

Culley's legs were longer, so he reached her first. She was standing in the lily pond, in water up to her waist, at once a comical and a terrifying sight, with strands of hair and muddy water streaming down her face and a lily pad looped over one ear like a bedraggled beret. Her eyes were squinched up tight and her mouth was wide open, and she was bellowing, "Mommy! Mommy!" at the top of her lungs.

When Culley scooped her into his arms she burrowed her muddy little face into his neck and clung to him like a limpet. He stood there, up to his knees in cold water, breathing like a long-distance runner, holding her trembling body against his thudding heart and murmuring, "It's okay, honey, it's okay."

It was a moment or two before he remembered Elizabeth. He opened his eyes and saw her standing at the edge of the pond, looking frightened and lost, and felt a constriction in his throat that had nothing to do with the small pair of arms wrapped in a stranglehold around his neck. He said, "She's okay, just wet and cold and scared." And it sounded as if he'd swallowed half the pond himself.

"Here you go, honey, here's your mother," he murmured to the frightened child. But when he tried to pull her arms from his neck she resisted, afraid to give up the safe place, even long enough to transfer to another one. Culley looked at Elizabeth, and found himself drowning in eyes so dark gray they seemed almost black. The constriction in his throat grew tighter. "Your mommy needs you," he said huskily, peeling Wendy away from himself and thrusting her into her mother's arms.

"She's cold," Elizabeth said through her own chattering teeth. "She's shaking."

"Here, put this around her." Culley hauled his shirt over his head without bothering to unbutton it. As he tucked it around Wendy's quivering body, he could feel Elizabeth's eyes clinging to him as desperately as her daughter had hung on to his neck.

"Thank you," she said, mouthing the words inaudibly.

His own voice was a rusty croak. "She'll be fine."

"I know. But she could have—"

"I'll have it filled in," he said harshly. "First thing tomorrow."

She just looked at him. With his hands he could feel the shivers coursing through Wendy's small body, and he knew that some of them were Elizabeth's. He felt a sudden, overwhelming need to put his arms around them both and hold them until the shivers stopped.

"Don' *like* that water," Wendy said suddenly, and gave a prolonged, grumpy sniff.

Elizabeth hugged her hard and sighed, "Oh, baby."

"A nice warm bath will fix you up, squirt," Culley said, tweaking a strand of her hair.

Wendy glared at him. "Don' *want* bath!"

"Oh, Wendy."

"See, what'd I tell you? Good as new!"

Elizabeth was laughing, but when she looked at Culley he saw the tears. It seemed a natural thing to put his arm around her shoulders and give her a reassuring squeeze . . . and then to leave it there while they walked slowly back to the house.

Elizabeth didn't want that walk to end. She wanted to stay like that for a long, long time, with Wendy safe in her arms, Culley's arm a comforting weight on her shoulders, his body strong and solid at her side, his own unique man-smell in her nostrils. *Culley's* smell—clean, warm, woodsy. It was new and exiting, but somehow familiar to her, evoking phantom memories of joys never experienced, intimacies never shared. She wanted to close her eyes and drink it in, let his nearness fill all her senses.

"Can I take her for you?" They were at the foot of the stairs. Culley's arm was gone from her shoulders, leaving her feeling cold and unguarded.

She shook her head, shifted her burden and mumbled, "No, it's all right, I've got her. Thank you." She kept her eyes lowered, her face turned away, not wanting to let him see her vulnerability. She expected him to leave her then, but he came with her up the stairs, not touching her, but simply being there, so that she felt his presence with every nerve in her body. She couldn't explain what it had meant to her, just having him there, with her, sharing the fear, sharing the relief, giving comfort and strength. She'd always had to be so strong. She had always been so alone.

In the bathroom, she set Wendy down and turned on the hot water in the tub, ignoring her daughter's irritable whimpers. Culley stopped in the doorway, leaning awkwardly against the doorframe, as if he wasn't sure he ought to be there.

"I really don't know how to thank you," Elizabeth said over her shoulder as she adjusted the water temperature in the bathtub, keeping her face turned away from him, not looking, because she wanted to look so badly. She couldn't let him know that she found his naked torso incredibly appealing. It didn't have the hard, sculpted look of an athlete or a bodybuilder, just the natural contours of a healthy, well-proportioned man in his prime, slightly tanned, with a few freckles on each shoulder, and a light tracing of hair in the usual masculine pattern.

Oh, how she wished he would go! She was much too susceptible to him right now!

Culley shrugged and hooked his thumbs into the pockets of his jeans, unknowingly pulling the waistband a little lower, revealing a narrow band of slightly paler skin. "I don't know what for. You'd have been there in another second or two."

"I know, but—" She stopped, swallowing a sudden dryness in her throat as her gaze snagged on the sight of his belly muscles, moving in and out above the waistband of his jeans. Almost desperately, she turned to Wendy and began pulling her sodden T-shirt over her head. "The thought of losing her . . . if anything happened to her, I don't know what I'd do. That fear is always there, you know?" She shook her head. "I don't know if you can understand what it's like, since you aren't a parent—" She broke off suddenly, remembering what he'd told her such a short time ago, and turned to face him, clutching his shirt to her chest, feeling his pain in her own heart. "Oh, Culley, I'm sorry. I shouldn't have said that. I know you wanted—"

"It's all right," he interrupted quietly. "You're right. I'm not a parent." His voice was flat, not angry or dismissive, just . . . flat, and strangely gentle. And there was something about his stillness, something she couldn't understand; but it seemed to tug at her, drawing her in rather than shutting her out. She felt herself move closer to him, almost against her will.

"I didn't quite make it," he went on in that same quiet way. "Shannon was already pregnant when she found out about the cancer. She refused the therapy that would have prolonged her life in order to protect the baby. She held on as long as she could—sheer willpower, I think—but it just wasn't enough. She was five months pregnant when she died."

"Oh, no!" It was a cry of anguish, straight from her soul. Empathy and compassion overwhelmed her. She moved to him instinctively, wanting to touch him and offer him comfort. He wasn't Dr. Ward, noted scientist, or even her employer, now; he was just Culley, a man with gentle eyes and a wounded heart.

She had actually taken two steps toward him before she stopped, brought up short by an insurmountable barrier. She knew that she didn't dare touch Culley. Not now. Not like this. Not ever. Because she found his body so intensely attractive. Because she wanted to touch him, not merely in comfort, but in sensuous and erotic ways, with excruciating, tension-building slowness, and with a fierce and fiery passion. She wanted to touch him so badly she ached with it, and so she couldn't allow herself to touch him at all.

"I'm sorry," she said in a choked voice, and did an abrupt about-face, still hugging his shirt. When she discovered it, she turned again, just long enough to hand it to him and whisper "Thank you." Long enough to recognize the loneliness in Culley's eyes, but not long enough, she hoped, for him to see the hunger in hers.

Wendy was whimpering and shivering pathetically. Elizabeth knelt and gathered her daughter close, murmuring soothing and sympathetic phrases as she undressed her and lifted her into the nice warm tub. When she dared look around again, Culley was gone.

Wendy woke up from her nap with a fever. Although he agreed with Elizabeth that there was absolutely no scientific foundation for the notion that immersion in cold water causes illness, and that it was probably one of those unexplainable fevers children get sometimes, it made Culley uneasy. He couldn't help but feel the whole thing was his fault.

Although he had an idea Elizabeth felt the same— that it was her fault. She'd spent the whole afternoon with Wendy, reading to her, playing with her, even sitting in her room while she napped. Culley thought maybe she was feeling a little guilty about letting her daughter wander off and was trying to atone for not having paid better attention.

He had an idea she was also avoiding *him*, but he was much less certain about her reasons for that. He was well aware that it had disturbed her, having him there in the bathroom with her. He knew there could be all sorts of reasons for that too.

It frustrated Culley, not knowing answers. If he didn't know the answer to something, he felt compelled to search until he found it. Right now he wanted to know what Elizabeth was thinking. He wanted to know more about her, how she felt about things, what made her tick. He already knew she was warm, loving, generous, compassionate, and maybe a little shy. He also knew it had only been a year since her husband had died. Was she still grieving? A year after Shannon's death, he remembered, he'd still been in a state of shock; but then, he knew that everyone handled grief differently and that everyone healed at a different pace.

It took a bit of self-discipline, but he did manage to tuck both Wendy's fever and Elizabeth's enigmas away in the back of his mind and spend a productive afternoon at his word processor. The house was so quiet and his concentration so intense that darkness came without his realizing it.

Hunger pangs brought him back. He looked around, startled to discover that it was night, and checked his watch to see if it was time for supper yet. He was stunned to find that it was nearly midnight.

As he was stretching the stiffness out of his muscles, he wondered why the cats hadn't come begging for their supper. Elizabeth had fed them, he supposed, but he wondered why Albert hadn't come in to say hello and take up his favorite napping place on the windowsill. As he was leaving his office to go downstairs in search of something to eat, he discovered that a heavy piece of cardboard had been nailed over the cat door. He uttered a soft little "Huh!" of surprise and thought, Now why in the world did she do that?

He was still pondering that as he passed through the upstairs hallway, so he didn't notice that both Elizabeth's and Wendy's doors were open, and the lights still on.

In the kitchen, he drank a glass of milk and ate a cold baked potato standing in front of the refrigerator with the door open. Then he looked in on Prissy and the kittens, turned out the lights and went back upstairs, yawning. He was tired, and that xenon was probably going to be waiting for him in the lab in the morning.

He'd taken off his glasses and emptied his pockets and was heading for the bathroom when he noticed the lights, and the open doors. Because he was concerned about Wendy's fever, he went to investigate.

In Elizabeth's room he found some clothes on a chair and an empty, unrumpled bed. Smiling to himself, he tiptoed into Wendy's room, knowing exactly what he'd find. Sure enough, there was Elizabeth, curled up on the foot of her daughter's bed in her blue bathrobe and bare feet, sound asleep, her soft, even breathing a gentle counterpoint to Wendy's peaceful snores.

Still smiling, Culley strolled over to the bed and stood looking down at them, mother and child. He touched Wendy's forehead, and then one cheek with the backs of his fingers. Good, he thought, no more fever.

Not smiling now, he turned his gaze back to Elizabeth. His fingers ached with the desire to touch her.

And why not? he thought. She was sleeping so soundly that she'd never even know. So he lightly brushed one cheek with the back of his forefinger, then hooked a tendril of hair and stroked it behind her ear. A little shockwave of emotion rippled through him.

She barely stirred when he picked her up, just sighed and settled against him as if *he* were the comfortable bed. Culley, on the other hand, felt anything but comfortable. Tiny as she was, she was still a grown woman and therefore no insignificant burden. But even more disturbing was the way she felt in his arms, and the natural way she'd fitted herself to him so that the feminine contours of her body lay warm and soft against his. The way her hair tickled his mouth and chin, so that it seemed a natural thing to do, to press his lips against the lemon-scented softness of it.

She'd chosen the room with the alcove and the bay window, the one he and Shannon had thought of using as a nursery. Her bed was a daybed, the kind with wrought iron on three sides, and a trundle bed underneath. And it occurred to Culley when he went to lay her down in it that he'd made a slight miscalculation. She was facing the wrong way. If he put her down, her head would be at the foot of the bed, and her feet would be on the pillows.

It's okay, he said to himself as he stood there frowning at the bed. I'm a scientist. I design systems for interstellar space travel. I can figure this out.

He turned around and sat down on the bed. So far so good—at least her head was pointing in the right direction. Now all he had to do was shift her off his lap and ease out from under her. Preparing to do that, he put his hands on her waist.

Elizabeth muttered indistinctly and put her arms around his neck.

Culley closed his eyes. Now what? His chest felt as if he'd just swallowed a slug of thirty-year-old whiskey.

"Elizabeth," he whispered hoarsely as he tightened his hands on her slender waist. "Hey, come on, you can let go, now. You're home."

"Culley?" She sounded inebriated. Culley chuckled with relief and looked down into her face. Her eyes stared back at him, sultry and surprising as a summer rainstorm. The fiery heat in his chest expanded until there wasn't room to draw a breath.

He knew what was going to happen, and he made no move whatsoever to stop it.

Six

"Culley?" Elizabeth said incredulously. He was so deliciously near, his breath warm on her lips. They tingled with the anticipation of his touch.

How sweet it was to wake with the feel of his neck under her palms, the silky brush of his hair across the backs of her fingers, the hard ridges of his thighs under her bottom. And exquisitely, in the narrow gap where the front of her bathrobe had come open, his thumb, stroking velvet shivers into her stomach.

Still barely awake, not thinking, only *feeling*, Elizabeth brought her chin up and touched her parted lips to his. Their breaths checked, gently merged, and then his lips began to move over hers, silk on satin . . . slowly, slowly, and with quivering reserve. Delight touched her like a spring sunrise, making her smile. Trembling with the joy of discovery, she felt his mouth respond to her smile, and held her breath while his tongue lightly traced the shape of it. She let go a tiny gasp when he slipped it between her parted lips.

And suddenly Elizabeth was fully, vibrantly awake, with desire coiling and writhing inside her, her breathing rapid and deep. In response to the spontaneous arch of her back and the lift of her ribcage,

Culley moved his hands up and down her sides, his thumbs discovering, then widening the gap in her robe. Her fingers tightened on the back of his neck, then crept upward into his hair. She lifted herself into his kiss with mindless abandon, wordlessly inviting his hands to come inside her robe, to slip around her body, to stroke her back, her sensitive underarms, the sides of her breasts. When his thumbs found her taut, tender nipples she moaned, and moved sinuously under his hands.

His mouth . . . his hands . . . how good they felt! How wonderful it was to be touched with that special blend of sensitivity and passion, of bone-melting eroticism and tender restraint. Hungers she hadn't even been aware of blossomed and swelled inside her, hungers she heard echoed in the groan that came from deep in Culley's chest.

When he pulled away from her she gave a tiny whimper and turned her face into his neck. He said her name once in a voice that sounded torn, pulled the edges of her robe together, and shifted his hands to her shoulders.

Elizabeth gave a long shaky sigh then, because she knew reason was returning, and she didn't want it to. Not now, not yet. For a little while longer, she prayed, just let me forget how impossible this is. It felt so *good*.

"Elizabeth," Culley said again, clearing his throat.

She nodded and pushed herself away from him, keeping her eyes lowered and one hand on the front of her robe. "I know. I know, I'm sorry. I don't know what—"

"Don't be sorry. It was my—"

"No! No. It wasn't you." She gave a rueful little laugh that was almost a sob, and tried to shift herself off of his lap. Her movements felt jerky and uncoordinated. "It was me. I woke up and . . ."

He held her shoulders, forcing her to stay where she was. "It was both of us." His expression was trying to be stern and somber, but somehow, without his glasses his face seemed oddly defenseless.

He sighed and said, "Elizabeth, what are we going to do about this?" His voice was very soft, very gentle. Behind a sweep of dark lashes, his eyes were dark and still; it occurred to Elizabeth that his smiles seldom touched them.

She shook her head. Unable to bear looking into his eyes another second, she shifted her gaze downward and fastened it with undisguised hunger on his mouth instead. Longing washed through her, so intense it rendered her mute; and in that long, electric silence her unspoken desires screamed like sirens.

She felt embarrassed, exposed, foolish. It had been all her fault; she knew that Culley had only been trying to be kind and considerate, carrying her to her own bed, and she'd practically attacked him— her *employer!* But the truth had come to her in those few moments, and she didn't know how to hide it. She wanted him. Her whole body ached with wanting.

"I—" she began futilely, and shook her head again. This time, by swallowing mightily, she was able to say, "It won't happen again, Dr. Ward, I promise."

He coughed and quickly agreed, "No, of course not."

Oh, but she wanted it to happen again!

With his fingers Culley tilted her chin firmly upward, forcing her to look at him. His smile was crooked and seemed strained. "Elizabeth, don't let this change anything. Please?"

"Change anything?" Too late! her heart cried. *She* was changed . . . irrevocably.

"Please don't be embarrassed. What happened was . . . Listen, it's understandable. We were both upset by what happened this afternoon. It's late, we're both tired. We were vulnerable, that's all." He was speaking slowly, searching her eyes as if looking for confirmation. She wondered which of them he was trying to convince. "But," he went on, his gaze wandering over her face, touching briefly and evocatively on her mouth, "we're both adults, and we have enough sense to recognize it for what it's worth, put it in it's proper perspective, and not let it interfere with our relationship. Don't you agree?"

"Oh," Elizabeth whispered. "Certainly." But her mind protested, *So, why am I still sitting here on your lap? Why is my heart still beating so fast and hard?*

Why were his hands still gripping her shoulders, his fingers absently stroking her back through the layers of cloth?

As if the same thought had just occurred to him, Culley suddenly eased himself out from under her and let go of her shoulders. She sank down on the bed; he stood up and raked his fingers through his hair. Then he looked down at her, opened his mouth, closed it again and shook his head.

After a moment it was he who said, "It won't happen again, Elizabeth. You don't . . . need to worry."

She clutched the front of her robe together and mumbled, "I'm not worried." Not about him, she thought, feeling chastened and wretched. It seemed that *he* was in complete control.

"Well. That's good." He hesitated, frowning. "I guess I'll say good night, then."

"Yes," Elizabeth said tightly. "Good night."

He went out, looking as if he had a perplexing scientific problem on his mind. Elizabeth sat where she was, holding the edges of her bathrobe together, rocking herself, wondering why she suddenly felt so frustrated, so angry, and so thoroughly miserable.

Culley went to bed angry and lay awake for a long time, staring into the darkness, listening to his body's frustrated twanging and trying to decide which he was angrier with himself about: What he'd done, or what he hadn't done. He was angry with himself for kissing Elizabeth, and he was angry with her for kissing him back. He was angry with his mother for saddling him with temptation, and angry with Elizabeth for being so beautiful and warm and spontaneous and responsive. He was even angry with Shannon all over again, for dying and leaving him. But most of all he was angry with himself for leaving Elizabeth.

Why not? He asked himself that at least a hundred times, lying alone in his bed with desire racing hot and undirected through his veins. Dammit, why not Elizabeth? For the first time since Shannon's death he'd found himself really wanting a woman, and what had he done about it? Made noble, platitudinous speeches like a Victorian schoolmaster, and taken himself off to his chaste and lonely bed!

For Pete's sake, he argued with himself, he'd been alone for five years. Five years was long enough. He was bound to meet someone sooner or later, so why not now? Elizabeth was a grown woman, a consenting adult. What went on between them was nobody's business but theirs. She'd been more than willing, and he knew that if he'd pursued that kiss just a little further, he wouldn't be alone in this bed right now with his loins aching and tension humming through all his muscles. The natural chemistry between them had already been well on its way to full-blown passion. And passion, Culley reflected sardonically, had no conscience.

And yet, he'd pulled back. Why?

Closing his eyes, he imagined Elizabeth in his arms, her soft white breasts pillowed against his chest, her gray eyes laughing down into his. "Idiot," he whispered, then groaned, opening his eyes again. He laughed silently and painfully into the darkness. Because, although passion might have no conscience, *he* did. And sooner or later, passion would be spent, leaving him with the cold, bitter knowledge that he'd taken advantage of a vulnerable, grieving woman who'd trusted him. No matter how he sliced it, it would be a lousy thing to do.

That knowledge made him feel a little better, but not much. The thing that calmed him, and enabled him to roll over, punch his pillow into submission and finally fall asleep, was the realization that he was, in the deepest part of his soul, a romantic. Something about Elizabeth must have struck that chord of romanticism in him, because he knew that he wanted more from her than a nice, lush body to warm his bed. He wanted her to respond to him, not because she was vulnerable and lonely and needing somebody, but because she wanted *him*. He knew that might take some time, but he was willing to wait.

The next morning when he came downstairs for breakfast Elizabeth and Wendy weren't in the kitchen.

His first reaction was disappointment. He'd gotten used to hearing, "Hi, Daddy!" when he walked into the room. He'd gotten used to the tangy scent of fresh-squeezed orange juice and seeing the morning sunshine through a cloud of red-gold hair.

His second reaction was a kind of bleak, regretful anger. She was avoiding him, of course, because of last night. He'd almost expected it.

He decided he wasn't going to let her get away with it. Dammit, he'd enjoyed her company yesterday—hers *and* Wendy's. All right, he knew he hadn't been happy at first about the idea of sharing his home with a strange woman and a two-year-old child, but he'd gotten used to it. The fact was, he liked having them around. And he was darned if he was going to spend the next couple of months tiptoeing around his own home like a character in a French farce, trying to avoid Elizabeth just because he'd behaved like a jerk and scared her to death. This, he decided, was something that needed to be brought out into the open and dealt with. He and Elizabeth were both mature, intelligent people. They should be able to discuss the situation in a calm, rational manner.

With that thought firmly in mind, he went looking for her. He found her on the back porch, down on her knees beside a laundry hamper, sorting clean clothes. When he saw her, he forgot for a moment what he'd come for and just stood there monitoring the odd new feeling in his chest with mild surprise.

When she saw him, she said, "Oh, hi," and looked as guilty as if she'd been caught red-handed laundering Mafia funds instead of socks.

Culley said "Hi," and squatted down across the hamper from her.

"See my sock?" Wendy lifted one foot, from the toe of which dangled one of Culley's argyles. Her grin and the sparkle in her eyes were a challenge.

Since he needed a moment or two to catch his breath anyway, he accepted the game good-naturedly. He cried, "Hey, that's *my* sock!" and snatched it from her foot.

Wendy shrieked, "No, mine!" and grabbed for the sock. Culley held it high over his head, just beyond her reach. Giggling and undaunted, Wendy hurled herself at him, knocking him flat on his back. With a squeal of delight and no regard whatsoever for ribs and abdominal muscles, she trampled over his belly, scaled his chest and trimphantly reclaimed the sock.

There ensued a small tussle, during which Wendy tried in earnest to stuff the sock down Culley's throat. It ended when, above his own yells of "Hey, you win! I give up! Uncle!" he heard Elizabeth's firm, no-nonsense voice say, "Wendy, that's enough. Let Dr. Ward get up now."

She lifted Wendy off him and set her, protesting, on her own feet. Culley stood up, brushed himself off, and dragged a hand through his hair. At least, he thought, now he had a good excuse for being distracted and out of breath. She'd never know that the minute he'd laid eyes on her his imagination had put her right back in his arms again. He could feel her there now, as if every square inch of his body had been imprinted with its own memory of hers.

"Well," he remarked, "she doesn't seem any the worse for her dip."

"Oh, no, she's fine." Elizabeth lifted the hamper onto the washing machine and went back to folding clothes. He moved closer to her, noticing the little stress frown between her eyes, the tense set of her shoulders.

"No more fever?"

"No, doesn't seem to be." She seemed to be avoiding his eyes. "Uh, listen, I left your breakfast in the oven to keep warm. I hope french toast is all right. Orange juice is in the refrigerator. I know you're probably in a hurry—"

"I'm not in a hurry," Culley said gently. "And I'd like to talk to you." He paused to clear his throat, momentarily thrown off course by the sight of her slender hands carefully smoothing the wrinkles out of his briefs. "About last night . . ."

Her hands stilled. "I see." He heard the soft sigh of her exhaled breath as her shoulders lifted and settled. "I guess you'd like me to leave as soon as possible. I understand."

Culley's gaze snapped to her face, but she was still looking down at her hands. Her lashes made bluish shadows on her pale cheeks. With his new emotions bouncing around inside his chest he rasped, "The hell you do!" Startled eyes met his. "What are you talking about? I don't want you to *leave*, dammit, I just want to talk!" Which was a lie. Right this minute what he wanted to do was take her in his arms and pick up where he'd left off last night.

Elizabeth was looking pointedly at Wendy, who

America's most popular, most compelling romance novels...

Here, at last...love stories that really involve you! Fresh, finely crafted novels with story lines so believable you'll feel you're actually living them! Characters you can relate to...exciting places to visit...unexpected plot twists...all in all, exciting romances that satisfy your mind and delight your heart.

EXAMINE 6 LOVESWEPT NOVELS FOR

15 Days FREE!

To introduce you to this fabulous service, you'll get six brand-new Loveswept releases not yet in the bookstores. These six exciting new titles are yours to examine for 15 days without obligation to buy. Keep them if you wish for just $12.50 plus postage and handling and any applicable sales tax. Offer available in U.S.A. only.

☐ **YES,** please send me six new romances for a 15-day FREE examination. If I keep them, I will pay just $12.50 (that's six books for the price of five) plus postage and handling and any applicable sales tax and you will enter my name on your preferred customer list to receive all six new Loveswept novels published each month *before* they are released to the bookstores—always on the same 15-day free examination basis.

40311

Name_____

Address_____

City_____

State_____ Zip_____

My Guarantee: I am never required to buy any shipment unless I wish. I may preview each shipment for 15 days. If I don't want it, I simply return the shipment within 15 days and owe nothing for it.

R82

Get one full-length Loveswept FREE every month!
Now you can be sure you'll never, ever miss a single
Loveswept title by enrolling in our special reader's home
delivery service. A service that will bring you all six new
Loveswept romances each month for the price of five—and
deliver them to you before they appear in the bookstores!

Examine 6 Loveswept Novels for

15 days FREE!

(SEE OTHER SIDE FOR DETAILS)

Loveswept

Bantam Books
P.O. Box 985
Hicksville, NY 11802

Postage will be paid by addressee

BUSINESS REPLY MAIL

FIRST-CLASS MAIL   PERMIT NO. 2456   HICKSVILLE, NY

NO POSTAGE
NECESSARY
IF MAILED
IN THE
UNITED STATES

was wrapped like an octopus around one of Culley's legs.

"Baby," she said in a calm, clear voice, "would you like to go out and pick some oranges?"

Wendy shook her head and tightened her grip on Culley's leg. "Want to play wiss *Daddy*."

"Daddy—I mean Dr. Ward can't play with you now. He needs his breakfast. He wants some orange juice. Why don't you go see how many you can put in this bucket?"

Wendy was beginning to look mulish and Elizabeth was beginning to look frustrated when Culley had an inspiration. "Wait a minute," he said, taking the bucket himself, "I'd better do it. Wendy's much too *little* to pick oranges all by herself."

"I not! I'm *big!*"

"Oh Wendy," Elizabeth sighed, picking up her cue. "I don't think so. Culley's right, honey, you're too little."

Wendy's lower lip began to quiver. "Want to pick *oranges*."

"Well . . ."

"Go ahead, let her try it," Culley said, winking at Wendy, who began to hop in excited anticipation.

"Well, all right." Elizabeth relinquished the bucket with a show of reluctance and held the door open for her daughter. "Not too many, now," she called after her, then turned back to Culley, looking sheepish.

"I thought we played that rather well," he said smugly.

She gave a spurt of rueful laughter. "We did. It was so easy I almost feel guilty."

"Amazing what a little teamwork can do, isn't it?"

Her smile faded quickly. "You wanted to talk to me?"

"Yeah," Culley said on an exhalation, hating the fearful look in her eyes, hating himself for having put it there. "I do. I think we need to talk, don't you?"

She turned away from him, making a pretext of straightening already immaculate piles of clean clothes. "I thought we did that." Her voice was muffled. "Last night."

Culley moved up behind her. "I thought we did, too," he said gently. "I thought we agreed you wouldn't be embarrassed."

She gave a little sniff. "That's easy for *you* to say."

"Look, Elizabeth"—he lifted his hand, and kept himself from touching her only by sheer effort of will—"I don't understand. Why are you so embarrassed about this?"

She turned to stare at him. "You've got to be kidding."

Culley dragged a hand through his hair. "Look, I kissed—" Seeing the expression on her face, he quickly put up his hand. "All right, all right, you kissed me." He paused for a moment, then quietly repeated it, holding her eyes with his. "You kissed me. What's so terrible about that?"

Elizabeth, it isn't terrible, at all. And I did kiss you. You kissed me. We kissed each other.

He heard the whisper of her exhaled breath. "I'm your housekeeper," she said, as if that explained everything.

Frustrated, because to him it explained nothing at all, Culley barked, "What's that got to do with anything?"

Her shoulders lifted and settled. Her body's lines seemed almost a caricature of vulnerability and misery. "You've been so nice to me, to us. And I practically attacked you!"

"The hell you did!" And then, very softly, "I didn't exactly fight you off, Elizabeth."

She turned slowly to face him. Her eyes caught at him, clung to him. He realized she was confused, and he was making it worse. He really had to give her more time.

"It's all right." He wanted to put his hands on her

shoulders, but thought better of it. It was putting his hands on her that kept getting him into trouble. "Listen, I know you're susceptible right now. Believe me, I understand. I've been there myself, remember? Give yourself a little time."

She gave her head a slight shake. "Time for what?"

He allowed himself the briefest of touches, just the pads of his fingers lightly brushing her cheek. "For grieving. It's only been a year since your husband died. Healing takes time." His smile was understanding. "Listen, I was a basket case for a long time after Shannon died. But I can tell you, it does get better."

The light behind her eyes faded, leaving them flat and opaque. In a cool, brittle voice she said, "You think I'm grieving?"

Elizabeth, don't hide from it! he wanted to yell at her. Don't close yourself in with your pain! Talk to someone. Talk to me!

"It's okay to be vulnerable," he said gruffly. "It's okay to need someone. A shoulder. I understand."

Very slowly she said, "Is that what happened, Culley? Is that what happened between us?"

He took a deep breath and lied, glibly and brightly. "Sure it was. You'd had a bad day, and you were in need of a little comfort, that's all." He gave her a determined smile. "You're making too big a thing out of it. Forget it."

Her mouth lifted in a wry twist. "What about you? Have you forgotten it?"

With her quiet eyes probing his, Culley found his newfound facility for lying slipping away from him. He looked back at her and felt the silence envelop them both like a warm summer night. He could almost feel her breath on his lips, her hands on his neck, her breasts against his chest. He felt as transparent as glass.

"Elizabeth," he said, lifting his hand toward her.

The front doorbell pealed, its foghorn echoes reaching them even on the back porch.

Culley muttered, "Damn!" Elizabeth closed her eyes and turned her head quickly to one side.

They waited in silence until it came again, and then Elizabeth said thickly, "I'd better go see who that is."

Throwing a quick look out the window at Wendy, who was still happily pulling oranges off the tree, Culley followed Elizabeth back through the kitchen and down the hall. He got to the front door just in time to see her greet the middle-aged couple on the doorstep. And to watch all the blood drain out of her face.

In a thin little voice he'd never heard her use before, she said, "Maggie . . . Carl. How did you— what are you doing here?"

Elizabeth felt Culley come up behind her and she shifted instinctively, moving fractionally closer to him. She wasn't sure whether or not she'd imagined the brief, reassuring pressure of his hand on her back, but it seemed to inject strength into her spine nevertheless.

"Why, Elizabeth," Margaret said with determined brightness, "we've come to see our little granddaughter, of course. Where is she? Where's my angel?" She was wearing her mink jacket, Elizabeth noticed, and at eight o'clock in the morning her blond hair was an artful tumble of stiffly sprayed curls.

"We were in the neighborhood," Carl drawled placidly, looking beyond Elizabeth's shoulder as he tucked his pipe into his coat pocket. "You must be . . ."

"Dr. Ward," Elizabeth murmured, still a little out of breath from shock. "This is Mr. and Mrs. Resnick. My . . . uh, Wendy's grandparents."

"Nice meeting you." As Culley reached past Elizabeth to take Carl's hand, he put his left hand on her shoulder, a gesture that wasn't lost on the Resnicks. Elizabeth saw the creases at the corners of Carl's eyes deepen slightly in speculation.

"Dr. Ward, my pleasure," he said in that deceptively jovial rumble of his. "Understand you're making some waves over at Cal Tech." Culley looked mildly surprised. Carl chuckled. "Did a little checking. Had a look at some of your articles on beta decay. Didn't understand a word of it, of course, but the Nobel committee must have been impressed. Congratulations."

Culley muttered something unintelligible. He was looking acutely embarrassed, and Elizabeth wanted very much to hear more, but Margaret had linked arms with her and was asking in a strident voice, "Where *is* Wendy? Oh, you know, I just can't wait to see my baby. It seems like ages. How's she doing, is she all right?"

"She's fine," she said through cold, stiff lips.

"She's out in the back yard picking oranges," Culley said, glancing at Elizabeth. There was a puzzled look in his eyes. "Come in. Elizabeth—"

"Oh, are you *sure*?" Maggie turned a look of wide-eyed appeal on Culley. "I know it's a bad time. We're putting you out."

Elizabeth gave a helpless shrug and looked at Culley. As usual, in confrontations with her in-laws, she was feeling invaded and outmaneuvered. And as control of the situation slipped away from her, she felt herself growing resentful and sulky. Childish, she told herself. She was being childish. The Resnicks loved Wendy. They meant well. She was all they had left of their son. How could she resent them for wanting to see her?

"Dr. Ward, if you need to leave, don't let us hold you up," Carl put in, looking sincere.

"Not at all," Culley said cordially. "Right this way."

Through the kitchen windows Elizabeth could see Wendy, still playing under the orange tree. She'd gotten tired of picking oranges, apparently, and was amusing herself by taking all the ones she'd picked out of the bucket and lining them up neatly on the grass. In her yellow sleeper, with her silky yellow hair falling over pink cheeks, she made Elizabeth think of springtime, and flowers, of buttercups and daffodils.

She's so beautiful, she thought, aching inside, overwhelmed by a wave of maternal love. She looked so small and unprotected. Elizabeth wanted to get to her first, to prepare her for her grandparents' visit, but Margaret, with her usual insensitivity, simply bulldozed her way through the back door and descended on Wendy with outstretched arms, trilling, "Oh, there you are! How's my Wendy? Come on, sweetheart, say hello to Grandma!"

Wendy's face went blank with shock, then crumpled. She took several steps backward, instinctively retreating, bumped into the bucket, knocked it over and sat down on its side. The bucket rolled forward, dumping Wendy ignominiously on her backside in the grass. Frightened and humiliated, she shut her eyes tightly and began to bellow.

Elizabeth clamped a hand over her mouth to hold back her own anger and dismay, while Margaret paused, looking taken aback. Culley calmly stepped around them both, picked Wendy up and dusted off the seat of her sleeper, then set her on her feet. "There you go, kitten, you're fine," he murmured, kissing her tear-streaked cheek. "Don't cry now, you've got visitors."

He ruffled her hair and started to straighten up, but before he could, Wendy clamped herself onto him, doing her octopus imitation again, both arms wrapping around his neck, legs hugging his waist. Finding Elizabeth's eyes over the top of Wendy's head, Culley shrugged as if to say, "What are you gonna do?" and stood up with Wendy in his arms. Once again, Elizabeth's breath seemed to catch in her chest.

The awkward moment was saved by Carl, who moved up next to Culley and tickled Wendy's cheek. "Hi," he said softly, "want to come and see Grandpa?"

Wendy considered for a few moments, then reluctantly unwound her arms from Culley's neck and transferred them to Carl's. He spoke quietly in her ear, saying something that made her giggle. Margaret fortified herself with a deep breath, then moved up beside her husband and patted Wendy's back. When Wendy accepted that with reasonably good grace, Elizabeth breathed a sigh of relief. She actually felt sorry for Margaret. She supposed the woman couldn't help being born without a nurturing bone in her body.

"Wendy," she said brightly, "would you like to show Grandma and Grandpa the baby kitties?"

Carl and Margaret, of course, greeted that suggestion with enthusiasm.

"Oh my goodness, Wendy, do you have kitties?"

"Can you show us the kitties, Wendy?"

Wendy nodded and said solemnly, "Baby kitties. I show you. Com 'ere." Carl put her down and offered her his index finger, and they all went back into the kitchen.

Elizabeth began to relax a little. It hadn't been as bad as she'd expected, and she couldn't help but wonder if Culley's presence had anything to do with that. She didn't quite know why or how, but she felt stronger having him there, even though he said very little, but stood quietly on the perimeter of things, looking on with calm, watchful eyes. Almost, Elizabeth realized suddenly, as if he were standing guard.

It was a fantasy, she knew, but she drew comfort from it nevertheless.

While the Resnicks were bending over the cat's box, oohing and aahing at the kittens, Elizabeth bustled around the kitchen, setting out cups and spoons and napkins and pouring coffee. And it occurred to her as she did so that there was nothing like an invasion of strangers to make her realize how much she was coming to think of it as her kitchen.

That was a fantasy, too, of course, but it gave her strength nevertheless.

And a few minutes later, when Margaret cleared her throat and said portentously, "Elizabeth, dear . . ." she knew she was going to need all the strength she could muster.

". . . Carl and I," her mother-in-law went on, giving her husband a conspirator's glance, "have been wondering about Thanksgiving. Now, I know you may have plans and, well, commitments, with your new job"—she paused to bestow a martyr's smile on Culley—"and everything. But the holidays are going to be so very difficult this year for all of us—" She pressed her fingertips to her lips and cleared her throat. "Well. Since Carl and I will be alone, we'd like to have Wendy come spend Thanksgiving with us, if that's all right with you."

"Of course, we'd like to have you both," Carl put in in his quiet way, "but if you have obligations, we certainly do understand."

As soon as Margaret had mentioned the word Thanksgiving, a vision had flashed through Elizabeth's mind. As clearly as if she were watching a movie, she saw herself in this kitchen, bending over to lift a huge, golden-brown turkey from the oven. She saw Culley come to help her, saw them both bending over the turkey, laughing as Culley sneaked a bite of stuffing, both of them reaching, with the instinctive vigilance of parents, to shield Wendy's questing fingers from the hot pan. She saw Culley lift Wendy up so she could see . . .

"Mommy, look at me!"

"Thanksgiving," Elizabeth said, rubbing her eyes. "Well, I was sort of planning—"

"After all, dear, you will be busy, I'm sure, fixing dinner for Dr. Ward. You know Carl and I will give Wendy all our attention, and Hilda always does such a marvelous job with the turkey."

"Mom-mee, look at me."

Margaret sighed. Elizabeth tensed. "Carl and I are alone now, you know. Wendy is all we have left of Kevin—" Margaret's voice broke.

But she's not Kevin! Elizabeth wanted to shout. And she's not your little girl! She's mine!

"Mom-mee!"

"Wendy, please. Oh my heavens!" Elizabeth leaped up just in time to rescue the kitten her daughter was wearing proudly on top of her head. "You know you're not supposed to hold the kittens up high," she scolded distractedly, keeping a firm grip on Wendy's arm as she returned the kitten safely to its box. "What would you do if it fell, huh? Do you know what would happen if the kitty fell off of your head? It would die!"

"Now, Liz, honey—"

Wendy was looking bewildered. "Die?"

"It would get hurt," Elizabeth amended. "Very badly. Do you want the kitty to get hurt?"

Wendy shook her head. Her lower lip was beginning to quiver.

"Elizabeth, she's just a baby, she doesn't understand—"

"She understands when she's not supposed to do something," Elizabeth said between clenched teeth. She picked up Wendy and plunked her down in her chair. Wendy began, inexplicably, to bellow.

Margaret looked distressed. Elizabeth looked at Culley. From across the room his dark eyes studied her, narrowed slightly in a thoughtful frown.

"She's upset," Elizabeth said, feeling distraught herself.

"Well, of course she's upset. Poor baby. Here, angel, come to Grandma."

Wendy bellowed louder.

"Look, Wendy, Grandpa brought you a present. Would you like to see?" Carl reached into his coat and brought out a small stuffed mouse. "There now. What do you think of that?"

Wendy hurled it across the room.

Elizabeth recognized the beginnings of a full-blown tantrum. It was her fault, she knew; she'd handled Wendy badly. She always seemed to handle things badly when the Resnicks were around. Feeling like a complete failure, she mumbled, "I'll take her upstairs," and hauled her screaming daughter out of her chair. All she wanted to do was get out of that room full of stress and tension and go somewhere quiet, peaceful, safe. "Carl, Maggie, I'm sorry, but—"

"Well, we need to be going anyway," Carl said kindly, patting her arm. "Margaret? Ready to go?"

"Oh, Carl—"

"I'll show you out," Culley said pleasantly.

On the way to the front door Carl Resnick paused and turned around. "Oh, Liz, honey . . ."

She stopped halfway up the stairs and looked at him over her daughter's head.

"We'll be by to pick up Wendy around ten o'clock on Thanksgiving Day. How'll that be?"

"Fine," Elizabeth said dully. She saw Culley open his mouth and then close it again before she turned and continued on up the stairs with her sobbing child in her arms.

Culley was angry again, but it was different from anything he'd ever experienced before. He felt a cold, mean rage, and it made him feel slightly sick. He wanted to take Elizabeth by the shoulders and shake her until her teeth rattled—her teeth, or her backbone. Which she suddenly seemed to have lost completely! Incredible. His golden-maned lioness turning into a sniveling coward, right before his eyes! He couldn't believe it.

He kept asking himself why she let those people walk all over her like that. He couldn't answer the question himself, so he asked Elizabeth when he ran into her at the foot of the stairs a little later, as he was leaving for work.

She was just coming out of the kitchen with the basket of clean laundry. When he confronted her, she stopped, shifted the basket to one hip and said, "I beg your pardon?"

"I said, why did you let them have Wendy for Thanksgiving?" Her eyes fell away, and she moved past him without answering. "You don't want her to go, do you?" She started up the stairs. Cully drove his fingers into the hair he'd just finished combing, then brought his fist down hard on the newel post. "Dammit, Elizabeth, if you don't want her to go, why don't you tell them?"

She stopped, finally, and her body seemed to wilt. In a small, stifled voice she said, "How can I? They've lost their only child. How can I say no?"

"They're using that on you, don't you see?" She put one unsteady hand on the banister and continued her climb. "Dammit, Elizabeth," Cully shouted, "you lost someone too!"

She hesitated, then choked out, "You don't understand," and began to run up the stairs. Culley knew by the sound of her voice and the way she moved that she was crying.

Culley's emotions were tearing him apart. Part of him wanted to go running after Elizabeth, tell her he was sorry, wrap her in his arms, comfort and protect her, make the hurt go away. Part of him was still too angry with her to think about touching her. But another part of him knew that even without the anger he had no business touching her—and that was the worst frustration of all.

Seven

When Culley walked into the lab, his assistant looked up and drawled, "Tough mornin'?"

Culley grunted, dumped his briefcase onto his desk and stared at it.

Mark Ellerman was a graduate student, dark, good-looking, and pushing two hundred and sixty pounds. He'd been Culley's lab assistant for almost a year and a half and was used to most of his moods, so he merely swiveled on his stool and said, "The xenon came in."

"Hmm," Culley said. He focused a frown on the briefcase, then shifted it to Mark and asked abruptly, "Are you married?"

That was a new one, but Mark was unperturbed. "Sure am."

"Any kids?"

"Yep." He held up two fingers, anticipating the next question, and added, "One of each—Brent's two and Jessica's almost four."

Culley frowned and said, "Hmm" again. Mark just waited patiently, ready to field another question.

"Do we have a phone book, one with yellow pages?"

"Sure do," Mark responded cheerfully. "In the desk. Lower lefthand drawer. What do you need?"

Culley looked up and said, "I'm not sure. Who do you call if you want a fishpond filled in?"

Mark didn't bat an eye. "That's easy. My brother-in-law, Ernie. No, I'm serious. He operates a back-hoe. He can get you a dump truck load of topsoil any time you want. When do you need it?"

"Yesterday."

"No problem. I'll call him at lunchtime. Probably catch him in then." Mark eased his bulk off the stool. "I'm going to the coffee machine. Want some?"

"Yeah . . ." Culley got his attention zeroed in on his departing assistant long enough to call, "Thanks a lot, Mark, I owe you one," and then went back to frowning absently at the telephone.

Presently, he picked it up, dialed information, and asked if there was a Carl Resnick listed in the Los Angeles area. There was—in Brentwood. He jotted the number down on a scratch pad, depressed the button, and dialed. And depressed the button again. After a few minutes he cradled the receiver and leaned back in his chair, letting his breath escape in a long exhalation.

It would be so easy to get her off the hook, he thought. He could simply call the Resnicks and tell them Elizabeth had other plans for Wendy's Thanksgiving, and that would be that. And nothing would make him happier. But Culley knew that slaying her dragons for her wasn't doing Elizabeth any favors. Like it or not, those people were a part of her life. They were her child's grandparents, they were always going to be, and sooner or later she was going to have to learn to deal with them. There was something about Elizabeth, he realized, that made him want to dash off to her rescue like a knight in armor, but he just couldn't let himself do it. She'd have to find the courage to stand up to her dragons all by herself.

He was still sitting there scowling at nothing when Mark came back with the coffee, but it wasn't his decision concerning Elizabeth and the Resnicks that had him wallowing in perplexing thoughts. Confident that he'd made the right decision, he could put that particular problem out of his mind. What he was doing was wondering when in the world he'd begun to think of Elizabeth's problems as his business.

Wendy had had a bad dream. She couldn't even remember what it was about, but it had scared her, and made her cry. She felt small and lost and cold, and even her Winnie-the-Pooh night-light didn't make her feel better. She wanted to go and get in bed with someone big and strong and warm. Someone who would make her feel safe and protected from the half-remembered scary things.

Sometimes, when Wendy was cold or frightened in the night, she went and got in bed with Mommy. But tonight, for some reason, thinking about Mommy didn't make her feel very safe.

Wendy didn't remember ever feeling so lost and small in her life. If Mommy couldn't make her feel better, who could?

And then she remembered someone else. Someone whose eyes were always kind, someone whose voice made her feel warm and snuggly. Someone who was big, and strong, and never, never scared. *Daddy.*

So Wendy slid out of her bed and padded down the hall to the daddy's room, hugging her blankie for courage.

Elizabeth woke up with the feeling that something was amiss, so of course the first thing she thought of was that she'd overslept. When the clock on the nightstand had reassured her on that point, she collapsed back on her pillow to wait for the adrenaline surge to subside. That was when it suddenly struck her that there was no tousled blond head sharing the pillow with her.

Hallelujah! she thought. Wendy had actually spent the whole night in her own bed for a change! All that talking and reasoning and cajoling she'd been doing for the past week must finally be working.

Overflowing with tenderness and maternal love, ready to reinforce this wonderful achievement with hugs and kisses and lavish praise, Elizabeth bounced out of bed and went to see if Wendy was awake yet.

Wendy wasn't in her bed. Most of the covers were trailing off onto the floor, but Wendy was gone, and so was her blankie. That was strange, Elizabeth thought, because although Wendy wouldn't go to sleep without her security blanket, she wasn't one to drag it around with her when she was awake.

Oh damn, she thought.

Calling softly so as not to disturb Culley, Elizabeth looked in the closet, behind the curtains, under the bed, every place, in fact, that a two-year-old could possibly be and in a few impossible places as well. Such as dresser drawers. She went into the bathroom and did the same thing. Then she looked in her own room again, on the off-chance she might have missed her.

Wendy wasn't there.

Determined not to panic this time, Elizabeth stood in the dusky hallway listening to the early morning silence, trying to think like a two-year-old.

The first thing she thought of, of course, was the office in the attic, that roomful of wonders Wendy still called the toy room. Culley had worked until very late last night, she knew; she supposed he might have forgotten to lock it.

But when she checked it, she found the door securely locked and the cat door nailed up tight. Even a spider couldn't have gotten in there without a key.

All the other bedroom doors were closed, their doorknobs too high and stiff for Wendy's baby hands.

That left only downstairs. Elizabeth found herself tiptoeing as she went through the silent house. She could hear her heart thumping painfully against her ribs. It was so *quiet!*

In the chilly kitchen, Prissy jumped from her box and came to wind around Elizabeth's ankles, leaving her babies mewing in a frantic chorus. Obviously, Wendy hadn't been through there yet.

And now Elizabeth did panic. She raced through the house, opening and closing doors, calling, swearing, breathing in desperate whimpers. She kept saying to herself, She wouldn't go outside, she wouldn't go outside . . . would she? Damn those cat doors!

Wendy wasn't in the house.

Where would she go? Elizabeth asked herself, fighting back unthinkable fears. What would she do?

She thought of the oranges! Yesterday Wendy had tipped over the bucket and spilled all her oranges. Maybe . . . but no, Wendy wasn't under the orange tree, nor anywhere outside that Elizabeth could see. But it was a big yard, and there were so many places. . . . And just like that, the unthinkable became thought: The lily pond.

Cold in her cotton nightgown, bruising her feet on the gravel, Elizabeth raced around to the front of the house. The lily pond was unruffled and serene, just beginning to reflect the pinkish tinges of the November sunrise. A pair of mourning doves roosted undisturbed on the broken fountain. There was no sign of Wendy anywhere.

Shivering and distraught, Elizabeth stood in the driveway and tried desperately to think straight. It was such a big yard. She didn't even know whether or not the front gate was shut. She wasn't dressed. She was freezing to death, and her feet hurt. She couldn't go running around looking for Wendy like this. She'd have to get dressed first. Should she call the police?

Through the chaos in her mind one word kept resounding: Culley. She pulled the memory of his quiet eyes into her consciousness and focused on it as if it were a beacon holding her on course.

Culley would know what to do, she thought, sniffling and wiping her eyes on the sleeve of her nightgown. She'd wake Culley. He could help her look for Wendy. Culley would know what to do.

Feeling more in control already, Elizabeth ran around the house to the back door and into the warm kitchen, nearly tripping over Prissy, who was still begging for her breakfast. She took the stairs two at a time and finally came to a halt, breathing hard, at Culley's bedroom door. When there was no response to her timid knock, she gulped in air, wiped her face once more on her nightgown, let the air out, and grasped the doorknob.

Culley's room faced west, and didn't get the morning sunlight. It was dim and warm and quiet and filled with the intimate sound of a sleeping man's breathing. Elizabeth crossed the room on rubber legs, her steps becoming slower and slower as she approached the bed. When she got there, every ounce of strength in her body simply drained away, and she sat down heavily on the edge of it.

Culley was sprawled on his back, softly snoring. From the waist down he was covered by his blankets and bedspread; from the waist up, his only covering was Wendy.

She lay on his chest with her head tucked under his chin, sound asleep, her baby hair strewn like ribbons across his dusky skin. One of Culley's arms was outflung, the other curved around Wendy. Elizabeth looked at the dark, square, masculine hand that rested, fingers splayed and protective, on her small daughter's pink sleeper and whispered a tearful and shaky "Oh, baby."

She melted. She came unglued. Her heart turned over. Every cliché she'd ever heard, all true. With everything loose and liquid inside her, Elizabeth stretched out a trembling hand, intending to touch her child's downy soft cheek, and found that her fingers were drawn irresistibly to a harder, rougher plain.

When she touched Culley's whisker-stubbled chin, he stirred and moved slightly, so that her fingers found his lips instead. He murmured an unconscious "Hmm" against her fingertips that she felt as a prickling vibration all the way to the center of her body. And then his brow furrowed, his lashes fluttered. She snatched her hand away just before he opened his eyes.

"Oh," he mumbled when he saw her sitting there. His eyes widened, his head jerked up off of the pillows, encountered the alien object nestled just below his chin, and sank back again. "Hi." He lifted his free hand, let it rest briefly on Wendy's head, then touched Elizabeth's cheek with the backs of his fingers.

"Hey," he said wonderingly, "your face is wet. Are you crying?"

The only answer she could muster was a shrug and a tiny, watery laugh.

"Come on." Easing Wendy into the crook of one arm, in a completely spontaneous and unexpected gesture, Culley hooked his other arm around Elizabeth's neck and pulled her down onto his chest. "There now. What is it? Come on, tell me what's wrong."

Wrong? she thought. How could anything be wrong? Lying like this, with the heady scent of a warm, just-awakened man in her nostrils, the reassuring thump-thump of his heartbeat in her ear, his hand cupping the curve of her head while his fingertips rubbed gently back and forth over her scalp with a faint and soothing rasp.

"Damn, you're cold." His voice was thick with morning's huskiness. "You're freezing. What've you been doing? Come on in here. Get warm."

Come in here? Get warm? Oh, if only she could. What a wonderful thing it would be, to lie next to him in that special intimacy, with his arms holding her close, legs entwined, his body's heat permeating hers, warming her clear to her soul. Aching with longing, Elizabeth gave a little sobbing laugh, eased herself away from him and sat up, wiping her face with her hands.

Culley stared at her for a moment, then rubbed his hand across his eyes and laughed, silently and ruefully. "Sorry," he muttered, "I guess I'm not awake yet." He looked down at Wendy, then carefully rolled her off his arm. Wendy sighed, snuggled down into the covers and went right on sleeping. Culley sat up, adjusted the covers around his hips and leaned forward with his arms resting on his pulled-up knees. "I'm sorry," he said again, very softly, looking intently into Elizabeth's eyes.

Elizabeth shrugged and murmured something—she wasn't sure what. Culley nodded and went on looking at her. After a moment he said, "Where were you? Were you outside?"

She nodded and made a sound that was still more sob than laughter. "I was. I couldn't find Wendy. I never dreamed—" Her voice broke, and she finished the sentence with a hand gesture, taking in both Culley and the sleeping child.

"Hey," he said huskily, "I'm sorry. I should have let you know. I probably should have taken her back. I guess I was out of it. I worked pretty late last night. . . ."

"It's all right," Elizabeth said in a small, choked voice and closed her eyes on a warm flood of tears of relief, and of longing, and other emotions too intense and confusing to name.

"Don't do that." Culley's voice sounded like tearing cloth. She felt his hands on her face, wiping away tears; felt them slip down to her neck and curve around under her hair, and then tighten convulsively as he growled, "Come here."

And then somehow her face was buried in the warm hollow of his throat, and his fingers were tangled in her hair, holding her close, stroking her back while he rocked her gently and murmured comforting things in a low, gravelly voice. "Shh, it's all right . . . I'm sorry you worried . . . everything's all right now . . . please don't cry. . . ."

As her own trembling subsided, she became aware of a strange, tight vibration deep within him, and of the hard, heavy thumping of his heart. She realized that his skin was slick with her tears and that when she touched it with her lips, it tasted salty. She realized that her hand was resting on his abdomen and that her fingers were beginning to explore with a will of their own.

"Elizabeth." It was less than a whisper, a sigh breathed against her temple, felt more than heard. His arms tightened; she felt his fingers on her chin and obeying their silent command, turned her face upward. For an instant she felt his breath blow cool across her tear-glazed lips, and then his mouth covered them with warmth.

His lips were firm and satiny, the touch of his tongue a tender quest. Elizabeth held herself still, at first, so full of the wonder of it she was afraid even to breathe lest she burst the fragile rainbow bubble of her happiness. Soon, though, her mouth blossomed and opened of its own accord; her fingertips brushed his cheek and explored his jawline with trembling awe. And in certain parts of her body, dormant fires sprang joyfully and unexpectedly to life.

When the bubble did burst, it took a tumult to do it.

They both froze when they heard the racket outside in the driveway. Elizabeth was the first to recover. "Good grief," she mumbled, pushing herself away from Culley and straightening up, "what's that?"

Wendy popped out of the covers like a prairie dog from its burrow. On her knees, still wobbly and squinting, she chirped, "What 'sat, Mommy? Where goin', Mommy?"

Elizabeth was on her way to the window. Culley started after her, then thought better of it and drove his fingers through his hair, swearing under his breath as he tucked the covers back around his hips.

"Me too!" Wendy cried, scrambling off of the bed. "Wanna see too! Uppy, Mommy!"

Too bemused to demand the usual "magic word," Elizabeth lifted her daughter into her arms. Wendy immediately stabbed the window with her pointing finger and announced in delight, "That's a *truck!*"

Culley joined them at the window, finally, wrapping the bedspread around himself like a toga. He yawned and muttered obscurely, "I guess he wasn't kidding."

"That's a dump truck," Elizabeth said in astonishment.

Culley leaned over to look past her shoulder. "Yep, it sure is."

Elizabeth stared at him over Wendy's head. "What in the world is it doing here?"

"I invited it." He frowned, avoiding her eyes, and hitched his toga higher on his chest. "I just didn't know it was going to be here quite so early."

"I don't understand. What are you going to do with a load of dirt?"

He turned to look out the window again. His voice sounded muffled. "Fill in the fishpond."

"You're filling in the fishpond?" Elizabeth stared at his profile while she let that sink in. When she leaned over to set Wendy down, she could feel her pulsebeat in her eardrums. "You mean because of—"

"Because of what happened. Yes." He sounded abrupt, almost irritable. "Why are you so surprised? I said I was going to."

"Well, yes, but . . ." She faltered and finally improvised, "I didn't think you'd remember."

It was a lame effort at humor, and she expected him to smile, but the look he turned on her was somber, even austere. "I don't forget important things."

Important. She was silent for a moment, letting that soak in. "Yes, but filling in with dirt is so—" She stopped, afraid to say the word, permanent. Once again she substituted "drastic."

Culley's frown deepened. "Drastic? The damn thing was dangerous."

"But this is your home. And we're just—"

"Look—" His voice was brusque, even harsh. "You live here now. This is your home too. I didn't want you to have to worry about it all the time."

Elizabeth could only look at him, unable to express the wonder that was in her mind.

The silence grew loud and electric. Culley glanced down at Wendy, who was staring in awe at his toga, and ruffled her hair with the tips of his fingers. When his eyes came back to Elizabeth, she felt their touch on her skin, on her bare throat and arms and even on the parts of her body hidden beneath the folds of her nightgown, as if it were his fingers caressing her there instead. Then he turned abruptly and strode from the room. In a moment she heard the bathroom door close.

"Where's daddy goin', Mom?"

Elizabeth answered Wendy's inevitable question absently, staring out the window at the dump truck, hugging her white cotton nightgown tightly across her body. *I don't forget important things. . . .*

As the full significance of what Culley had done sank in, Elizabeth felt herself fill up and overflow, like a kettle coming to a boil. And of all the joys inside her at that moment, the most wonderful was the sense of belonging. She felt as if she'd finally made landfall after a long, exhausting sea voyage.

This is your home now.

With her self-esteem blossoming like desert flowers after rain, Elizabeth scooped Wendy up and danced with her, giggling and squirming, down the hall to her own room.

When he came downstairs after showering and shaving, Culley found Elizabeth and Wendy sitting on the front steps, dressed in warm sweatshirts and jeans, watching the last clods of dirt rumble from the truck and onto a pile of earth where the lily pond had once been. Wendy was sniffling dejectedly into her mother's shirtfront. Culley lifted an eyebrow at Elizabeth as he sat down beside them and ruffled Wendy's hair.

"What's the matter, squirt?"

Elizabeth turned her head toward him and murmured, "She's a little upset about the frogs."

Her eyes were shining, her cheeks touched with pink from the brisk morning. A breath of a breeze lifted a curling tendril of red-gold hair and laid it across her face. Culley had to stifle an urge to slip his finger under it and tuck it back into the warm place behind her ear.

He found himself suddenly remembering the way she'd looked a little while ago, sitting on his bed, eyes luminous and frightened, face wet with tears. He was remembering small things, like cold-hardened nipples in subtle relief under a white cotton night-gown, a nutmeg sprinkle of freckles on the rounds of her shoulders, the slight quivering he'd felt in her lips when he kissed her. Those things stirred him now as they had then—powerfully, physically, emotionally. How much longer, he wondered, would he be able to keep his hands off her?

"Hey, squirt," he said to Wendy, taking her arms and swinging her down from the steps while she was still too startled to protest, "forget the frogs. They'll find a new place to live. This is going to be great. Come on, I'll show you."

Dumbstruck with awe, gazing up at him with bright, trusting eyes, Wendy gave him her hand.

Culley led her across the gravel drive to the edge of the mound of earth. The dump truck was just pulling away, so they waved good-bye to the driver and waited for the rumble to subside, and then Culley squatted down beside Wendy and picked up a handful of rich brown soil.

"You know what this is?" he asked her, sifting the stuff from one hand to the other. "This is dirt. It's great stuff. Your mother's gonna love it. You can play in it, dig tunnels in it, do all sorts of things with it. Every kid should have nice clean dirt to play in." He glanced over at Elizabeth and saw that she was standing there watching them, laughing. Without taking his eyes from Elizabeth, he went on, "And later we'll plant some flowers. You can help. We'll plant pansies. Pansies are flowers with funny faces, did you know that?"

He was talking to Wendy, but for the life of him, the only face he could see was Elizabeth's, looking the way it had looked this morning, just before he'd covered her mouth with his.

Wendy commanded his attention then, and the next time he glanced over at Elizabeth, she wasn't there. She'd only gone back into the house, he knew, but somehow the morning seemed grayer and colder, as if the sun had gone behind a cloud.

When he was finally able to drag Wendy out of the dirt and back into the house for breakfast, he found Elizabeth in the kitchen, just hanging up the phone.

"Who was that?" he asked as he hoisted Wendy up to the sink, naturally assuming the call had been for either him or his mother.

Elizabeth turned to him, looking flushed and out of breath. "That was the Resnicks," she said. "I called them."

"Oh?" Culley waited, holding his breath.

She had a funny look on her face—triumphant, but a little frightened, too, as if she couldn't quite believe what she'd done. "I told them I've changed my mind. I told them I wanted Wendy to spend Thanksgiving with me."

Culley let his breath out and said quietly, "Bravo." And then he turned back to the sink and began methodically to wash Wendy's hands and face, hoping thereby to disguise the fact that what he really wanted to do was shout the word, and grab Elizabeth and hug her until her ribs squeaked. "How did they take it?" he asked casually, rescuing the dishwashing soap from Wendy's inquisitive hands.

"Not well." Culley glanced at her and saw that she was looking less radiant and more uncertain. "Is it all right? I mean, I don't know what you had planned for Thanksgiving. Do you want a formal dinner, you know, with family, friends?"

"Nothing fancy," Culley said. "Usually there's been just Mom and me. We don't have to do anything special. Don't go to any trouble."

But in his mind there was a picture, of himself and Elizabeth facing each other across the table in the dining room, her eyes reflecting candlelight, her hair like burnished copper, her lips parted and glazed with wine . . . lifting their glasses to each other across the perfectly browned turkey, while Wendy banged impatiently on the linen tablecloth with her spoon . . . and afterward, with Wendy napping peacefully upstairs, lying together in front of the fireplace in the den, making sweet, tireless love all afternoon long.

Eight

On Thanksgiving Day the telephone rang while Culley was helping Elizabeth clear the table. He answered it in the kitchen.

"Hello, Gregory," a tiny, distant voice said. "How are you, darling?"

"Who is this?" Culley winked at Elizabeth, who was just coming through the door with a load of dirty dishes.

"Don't be funny, Gregory. I called to wish you a Happy Thanksgiving."

"Thanks, Mother, that was very thoughtful of you." Elizabeth looked up from the sink to smile at him and mouth the words, "Say hello for me." He smiled back at her and nodded. "Where in the world are you calling from? You sound light years away."

"That's your thing, darling, not mine. I'm only in Tahiti."

"Tahiti!" Across the room, Elizabeth raised her eyebrows and mouthed the word, "Wow." Culley said, "I didn't know they had telephones in Tahiti."

"Well, there probably aren't many, and this is a fabulous luxury, so don't waste time with sarcasm, Gregory."

"Sorry, Mom." Culley chuckled. "I really am glad

you called. I got your postcard from Acapulco. Are you having a good time?"

"I'm having a wonderful time. I had no idea there were so many little islands out here. We've chartered a boat. I don't know why I didn't do this long ago." Culley winced at that. He knew why she hadn't done it before; she'd been worried about him.

"But listen, darling, I want to know how everything is. How is Elizabeth?"

"Elizabeth is fine, Mother. She's right here. She says hello." Elizabeth had given up any pretense of doing the dishes and was leaning against the sink, sharing the call with him. He found it an odd sort of intimacy.

"Oh, wonderful. Say hello for me, too. How is Wendy?"

"She's fine, too. She's upstairs, hopefully asleep." He looked a question at Elizabeth, who nodded vigorously and raised her eyes prayerfully heavenward.

"Give her a hug for me. She's such a sweetheart, isn't she?" *Hah*, Culley thought, *I wish you could have seen the tantrum she threw when we tried to drag her in off the dirt mound today!* "So, Elizabeth is working out all right, I take it? I assume you've discovered by this time whether or not she can cook."

"Oh yes," Culley said, winking at Elizabeth, "she can cook . . . pretty well." Elizabeth made a face at him and muttered, "Thanks a lot."

"Well, I'm glad everything's going well. I'm off for the outer islands. Oh! I almost forgot, I've changed my mind about Singapore."

"Oh," Culley said, surprised by a twinge of disappointment. "Does this mean you'll be back for Christmas after all?"

"Not at all. As a matter of fact, I've met this darling couple from Sydney—"

"Sydney, *Australia*?"

"That's right. And they've invited me to come for a

visit. So after New Guinea and New Zealand, I'm going to be staying on with them for a bit."

"I see," Culley said slowly.

"Don't worry, darling. I'm having the time of my life. I'll miss you, of course, but I know you'll have a lovely Christmas with Elizabeth and the baby. I think children just make Christmas, don't you? Well, good-bye, love, take care of yourself. I'll send you a post-card from New Guinea!"

"Thanks," said Culley absently as he hung up the phone.

Christmas with Elizabeth and the baby. It was the kind of thing he hadn't allowed himself to think about the last couple of weeks. In fact, he'd tried very hard not to think at all about Elizabeth, and to see her as little as possible, something he'd managed only by spending practically every waking moment either in the lab or in front of his word processor. He saw her only briefly in the mornings, and never alone. In the evening he usually managed not to come home until she'd gone to bed. They communicated by means of notes left propped on the hall table or secured by magnets to the refrigerator door.

And thank goodness, he told himself, there wasn't much danger of another one of those electrically charged, accidental meetings. The plumbing in both bathrooms was working fine, and Wendy's nocturnal ramblings had been curtailed. For her own peace of mind, Elizabeth had affixed a hook and eye latch to the top of Wendy's bedroom door.

Culley thought he must have asked himself a hundred times during those two weeks why he was doing this. Why, he wondered—usually in the middle of the night as he lay wide awake with all his senses humming in overdrive—was he going to so much trouble to avoid a beautiful, desirable woman with whom he obviously had a tremendous amount of chemistry?

Maybe he was being incredibly old-fashioned, the result, he whimsically hypothesized, of having spent most of his life in a Victorian house, but somehow, the answer always came up the same: It was just sleazy. He analyzed it over and over again. A vulnerable young widow with a child to support, struggling to get out from under the thumb of her overbearing in-laws, desperate for a job and a place to live, hired by the mother of a reputable scientist to be his housekeeper, and then seduced by said reputable scientist? *No.* No matter how he dissected it, it was still the same—sleazy. He might as well change his name to Snidely and wear a handlebar mustache.

And as many times as he ran the scenario through his mind, that was how many times he tried to come up with a way to change it; a way to circumvent his conscience, a way to justify doing what he wanted so badly to do—which was to take Elizabeth into his bed and make love to her all night long. And to make love in all the ways he knew—sweet and tender, slow and sensual, wild and fiery, giddy and playful. He wanted to feel her soft, slender body under him, her legs wrapped around him. He wanted to bury his face in her hair and himself in her tender warmth. He wanted to feel her gentle hands and sensitive mouth on his passion-heated body.

So far, he'd spent a lot of frustrating nights and had found no solutions. It was ironic, he thought, that he was a man who dealt on a daily basis with complex scientific and mathematical problems that would boggle the average mind, yet he couldn't solve the simplest of all human equations: One plus one equals two.

The best he'd been able to come up with was a vague idea that the situation would solve itself if he gave it enough time. Elizabeth's wounds would heal, as his had, and she'd be ready to risk a new relationship. She'd get stronger, learn to stand up to her in-laws. Eventually, his mother would come back and Elizabeth would move out of his house and get a decent job. In a lot of ways he was dreading that, but at least then he could court her as he longed to do. He would send her flowers, take her to dinner, dancing . . .

In the meantime, all he had to do was keep his hands off her. And the only way to do that, it seemed, was to keep away from her.

But in the meantime, there was Christmas.

It occurred to him that he didn't even know what Elizabeth's plans were for Christmas. He didn't know whether she had any family; she'd never spoken of any, except the Resnicks. He remembered that she'd said she was an only child. Funny, now he thought about it, how little he actually knew about her. The few times they'd talked, he'd done most of it; she'd seemed to love hearing about his childhood, about what it was like growing up in this house.

A vision took shape in his mind, bathed in the golden light of fireplace and candles: Wendy in red velvet and lace; Elizabeth in . . . green, he thought, something that would leave her creamy white throat and shoulders bare; himself, with one hand resting possessively on her shoulder, sipping eggnog from a crystal goblet. He could almost hear their laughing voices while carols played softly on the stereo. He could smell the warm, spicy smells of Christmas.

"What's the matter? What did she say?" Elizabeth asked, startling him. She had a concerned frown on her face. Culley realized he must have been standing there for quite a while, staring at the telephone.

"What? Oh, Mother says she's not going to be here for Christmas after all. She's going on to Australia."

"Oh," Elizabeth said softly, "I'm so sorry. I know you must be disappointed."

Culley stared at her for a moment, and then, realizing that she'd misinterpreted his pensive silence, shook his head and said quickly, "No, no, it isn't that. I was just thinking that I don't know what *your* plans are for Christmas."

Elizabeth shrugged and looked away. "I don't have any."

"What about your family?"

"Well, I don't really have any—except for my parents." She gave a nervous little cough.

"What about them?" Culley persisted, fighting frustration. She was shutting him out again, and his probing mind couldn't stand that. "Won't you want to spend some time with them?"

She threw him a look, and a sad, gentle smile. "No. I don't see very much of them."

There was a little silence, and then Culley said, "You don't like to talk about yourself, do you?"

Elizabeth looked a little surprised. "It's no big deal," she said with another of those dismissive shrugs, turning back to the dishes. "Nothing grim or anything. It's just that . . . my parents are getting along in years. They live in Phoenix now—my mother lives with her sister there so she can be near my dad. He's in a—" She coughed, and finished the sentence in a mumble. "—a home there. He wouldn't know me if I did go to see him, so . . . I don't."

Culley moved up beside her and picked up a dishtowel. Keeping his voice as casual as he could, he asked, "Alzheimer's?"

She nodded without looking at him. "It started when I was in high school. That's one of the reasons—" She paused and finished, "—I came to California to go to college." But Culley knew it wasn't what she'd started to say. "It was so *hard*," she said, laughing a little to cover the break in her voice, "to watch him deteriorate like that, you know? And my mother was distraught, trying to cover for him, trying to pretend it wasn't happening. I couldn't stand being around them." She shook her head and said flatly, "I still can't. So I don't. So . . ." She turned her head to smile brightly at him. "It's just me and Wendy."

"Well," Culley said, "I guess we're both pretty much on our own this Christmas." He was having to concentrate hard on the plate he was drying in order to keep himself from putting his arms around her. She has too many dragons, he thought. She shouldn't have to fight them all alone.

She flashed him a quick, uneasy look and murmured, "Looks like it."

"So . . . I guess we'll be spending it together. You, me, and Wendy." Elizabeth didn't answer, so Culley cleared his throat and said carefully, "I guess this will be Wendy's first *real* Christmas, won't it? I mean, she was just a baby last December."

She nodded, looking down at her hands where they rested motionless in the soapsuds. Culley could imagine what she must be feeling, facing the holidays without her husband for the first time, trying all by herself to make Wendy's Christmas special, when they must have had such plans. He laid the dishtowel down and put his hands on her shoulders, turning her to face him.

"I know it's tough," he said slowly, picking his words as if they were slippery stepping stones in a raging river. "I want you to know that I'll do whatever I can to make it easier for you." One slightly battered knight to the rescue.

Her eyes came slowly to his . . . huge, liquid, luminous. He felt himself getting lost in them. Trying desperately to keep his footing, he went on, "The thing to do is concentrate on Wendy. On making it a special time for her. Christmas is for kids anyway. We'll put up a tree, hang stockings, the whole bit. Hey, it'll be—" He stopped, because Elizabeth was shaking her head, backing away from him, pulling herself from his grasp.

"No, no, you don't understand."

"Elizabeth, I know you might not believe this, but I do understand. I've been—"

"No!" Her eyes had darkened in anger and pain. "You *don't* understand. Wendy won't even be here. I told—"

"The Resnicks?" Culley spoke softly, but inside him a little flower of anger was blossoming. Anger and disappointment.

She nodded. "I told them they could have Wendy for Christmas. It was the only way—" She took a deep breath and turned miserably away from him. "It was the only way I could get them to agree—"

"To *agree*?" Culley couldn't believe what he was hearing. "To agree to what? To let you keep your own child for Thanksgiving? Is that what you did? You bought one holiday at the price of another? What kind of a trade was that?"

"You don't understand, it's not that simple!" She whirled on him, her own anger her only defense against his. "Yes, I traded them today for Christmas. And I won't change my mind this time either. I can't. Because it's fair, Culley. It's fair. Of course they want to spend Christmas with Wendy! She's their grandchild. And the only one they're ever going to have. How can I possibly keep them from having this time with her?" She sniffed, beseeching him with her eyes.

And he felt ashamed, because he knew that in a way she was right. He knew how hard it must have been for her to give up her child for Christmas; he knew how torn she must be inside, and he ached for her. He just hoped the Resnicks appreciated the magnitude of the gift.

"Elizabeth, I'm sorry." Unable to help himself, he reached out to lay his palm against her cheek. Her eyelashes fluttered down upon unshed tears. "I'm sorry. I'm on your side, you know. I know how much you'd like to have Wendy with you for Christmas, and I guess my loyalties got in the way." His throat felt gravelly, so he cleared it. Taking his hand away from her face was hard, but he did it and tucked it safely between his arm and side. He said brusquely, "If you want to be with Wendy, you could always spend Christmas with the Resnicks too."

She shook her head, opened her eyes, looked briefly into his and then away, as if she found the sight of him painful. "No."

"If it's me you're worried about, don't. Hey listen, it's a holiday, remember? I'd hardly expect you to work on Christmas Day!"

"No. It isn't that. I'd just rather not spend Christmas with the Resnicks."

And that's that, her tone said. Subject closed.

There was an awkward little silence, and then Culley said, "So. I guess it's going to be the two of us then."

"Yes," Elizabeth said, "I guess so."

She was looking at him now, but Culley wished she wouldn't. In that long silence, gazing into those expressive eyes of hers, he began to feel as if he were on a sinking ship, bailing for his life with a teacup.

Of course, after Thanksgiving, the annual commercial Christmas blitz shifted into high gear; the shopping malls featured Christmas carols and animated models of Santa's workshop; television programming consisted of reruns of cartoon Christmas specials and exotic perfume commercials; and the mail seemed to be mostly requests for charitable contributions.

Elizabeth was having a hard time getting into the holiday spirit. She didn't know why. She kept telling herself how wonderful everything was, compared to last year, when she'd been in the midst of the worst part of the nightmare. She kept telling herself how lucky she was, how well her life was going right now, how happy she ought to be.

Two Christmases before she'd been living in a tiny apartment with a broken bathroom door where Kevin had put his fist through it. She'd been two months behind on the rent, and the phone had been shut off, and she'd had to hide her purse because she'd found out Kevin had been stealing money out of it to buy cocaine. Two weeks before Christmas, Kevin had taken her car and disappeared for three days. He'd turned up eventually—in jail—but in the meantime, Elizabeth hadn't had any way to get Wendy to the sitter's, or herself to work, and only the good-heartedness of her boss and the spirit of the season had kept her from losing her job.

Now she was living in a lovely old house, rent free; she had a kind, generous employer and a job that allowed her to keep Wendy with her. She wasn't dependent on the Resnicks. She was safe and secure. Sometimes it just seemed too wonderful to be real.

Last year, she'd taken Wendy to the mall to see Santa Claus and she'd screamed blue murder and refused to even look at him. This year, primed by storybooks and television, she'd climbed up on Santa's lap and flirted outrageously with him until the manager had had to suggest politely that it was time she gave the next kid in line a turn. Last year, Wendy had been pale and withdrawn and suspicious of strangers. This year she was healthy, happy, beautiful, and outgoing, and Elizabeth thanked God every day for her.

This year, she thought with a sigh, she wasn't alone, she was lonely. And she'd decided that the very worst kind of loneliness involved just one other person, being close to someone you cared about, and yet close only as in proximity, not as in union.

She didn't understand Culley!

And why should she understand him? She scolded herself mockingly. The man was a genius. Geniuses were supposed to be eccentric and unfathomable.

But sometimes late at night she lay awake, railing at the darkness in futile anguish: Why was he doing this to her? Why did he keep changing signals, confusing her so! Why did he look as if he was having so much fun when he was with her and with Wendy? Why did he make their business his business, and their problems his problems, as if he really *cared*? Why had he kissed her—twice!—and then acted as if nothing out of the ordinary had happened? Why did he sometimes touch her in those lingering, tender ways that made her whole body melt? Why, oh why was he avoiding her like the plague?

"Dr. Ward! What are you doing here so late?"

Mark Ellerman, on his way down the hall with a Santa Claus suit slung over his shoulder, paused to stick his head in the lab door.

"Mark, come on in," Culley sat back, stretched, and casually turned his writing tablet over, an automatic, and in this case unnecessary, precaution. All he was hiding was a perfectly legitimate article for the *American Journal of Nuclear Physics.*

"You've sure been putting in the hours lately," Mark commented, sitting down on a corner of Culley's desk. "Don't you know it's Christmas?"

Trying not to wince as the desk creaked under Mark's weight, Culley yawned and said, "Just thought I'd get a head start on my New Year's resolutions—that article the *Journal* has been begging for."

"Thought you had a word processor at home."

"I do. But I'm having my house painted," Culley lied, glibly and with true inspiration, "Fumes get to me."

"Yeah, yeah, I know how that can be." Mark's brow was furrowed.

"What about you?" Culley asked politely when Mark showed no inclination to move. "Why aren't you out Christmas shopping?"

It occurred to him suddenly that he had some of his own to do. As his mind wandered off on that tangent he thought that Wendy wasn't going to be a problem—all he had to do was get her some kind of toy—but what in the world could he get for Elizabeth? He knew what he would like to buy for her— something silky and sexy, soft as a lover's whisper, lavender, he thought, or maybe silver-blue.

How little he knew about her! he thought again, experiencing that special frustration she so often inspired in him. What were her tastes in clothes and jewelry? He realized he'd never seen her in anything except the jeans and sweaters or sweatshirts she wore around the house. Did she have a sweet tooth? A hobby?

"No," Mark was saying, heaving a sigh, "my wife takes care of most of my Christmas stuff. I just stopped by to pick up this thing." He lifted his finger with the Santa suit's hanger swinging from it.

"They roped you in again this year, huh?"

Mark chuckled ruefully and patted his expanding waistline. "Typecasting, I guess. Sure wish I could figure a way to get out of it, though."

"Why? I thought you got a kick out of it last year."

"I did. You know, I really did. If anything'll put you in the Christmas spirit, playing Santa for a bunch of sick little kids ought to do it, right? No . . ." He heaved another gusty sigh, hitched himself off the desk and swung the Santa suit back over his shoulder. "It's just, I've got kind of a family conflict, that's all. My little girl Jessica's church preschool is having a special Christmas Eve thing, and Jessie really wanted me to be there. It's a little bit ironic when you think about it, you know? I'm making all these other kids happy, and I'm breaking my own kid's heart." He started out the door and then paused suddenly, looking thoughtful.

"Dr. Ward?"

"Yeah?" Culley said warily, because he had a feeling he knew what was coming.

"Dr. Ward, I was just thinking . . . Did you mean it the other day when you said you owed me one?"

Elizabeth was in the library blatantly snooping. She'd been racking her brain to think of something to get Culley for Christmas, and had finally stooped to taking inventory of his desk drawers in the hope that the need of some clever accessory would become apparent to her.

She'd done all the rest of her shopping with no fuss at all. The coffee-table book of photos of the California seacoast had been mailed to her mom and dad in Phoenix. Carl Resnick's favorite brand of pipe tobacco and Margaret's favorite brand of perfume were already wrapped and ready to be delivered when she dropped Wendy off at their house on Christmas Eve. She'd probably end up getting a few more small things for Wendy's stocking, but the big gift, the important one, had been taken care of. She'd had a time trying to find the particular Solar the Antarian doll she wanted—most stores were sold out and had waiting lists for the next shipment—but she'd just happened to luck out at a discount store one day last week.

Which left only Culley. And with only a week to go before Christmas, she was at her wit's end.

The trouble with Culley, she decided, was that, like most men, he already had everything he'd be likely to want. And the ideas that did occur to her all seemed too personal. She'd thought of a new bathrobe, something soft and elegant in a warm, rich color like brown or magenta that would caress his skin as she could not. . . . She did have some whimsical notions inspired by that locked room upstairs, but of course she could hardly use any of those. Not without giving away her knowledge of his guilty secret.

Elizabeth was smiling to herself, thinking of the wonders in the attic, when she heard Culley come in. As always when she heard his step or his voice, her heart gave a joyful jump; to help herself deny that phenomenon she said peevishly to herself, "Well, miracle of miracles, he's home before midnight for a change!"

It was too late to keep him from knowing she was there; she heard his footsteps pause as he noticed the light on in the library. The way he'd been avoiding her lately, though, it was a surprise to her when the footsteps came across the living room floor.

"Hi," he said, sticking his head through the doorway, "what are you doing up at this time of night?"

"Just looking for something to read. I was having a little trouble getting to sleep." They were speaking in the hushed tones people use late at night, even when there's no one to be disturbed by their voices.

"Oh. Well, I hope you find what you're looking for. Guess I'll say good night, then."

"Good night."

He went on looking at her for a moment or two, then turned to go. That was when Elizabeth noticed that he had a Santa Claus suit on a clothes hanger dangling from one hooked finger. She was so taken aback by the sight that by the time she was able to formulate a question, he had gone.

She turned out the lights and made a side trip to the kitchen to check on the kittens, who had reached the stage where they were trying to climb out of their box. But tonight they were sleeping, peacefully and alone; Prissy was apparently out hunting in the moonlight.

With the house secured for the night, Elizabeth stood at the kitchen window, looking out at the night, listening to the quiet, trying to calm the yearnings of her body and soul. She thought about the house, and how warm and welcoming it had seemed to her at first, and how cold and lonely it was to her at this moment.

What had happened? she wondered. But she knew the answer.

Culley had happened. How, she still wasn't sure; she hadn't expected anything from him. All she'd wanted were a job and a safe, secure place for Wendy. She still didn't expect anything from him, how could she? She was just a housekeeper, and a temporary one at that. She was a twenty-six-year-old widow with a child, no money, no career prospects, no particular talents, not even a college degree, thanks to having dropped out of school to work full time soon after she and Kevin had married. And Culley was Dr. G. Cullen Ward. For heaven's sake, if Carl Resnick was right—and he always was—Culley had won a Nobel prize, or was about to!

No, she told herself dismally, she had no business having any expectations or yearnings where Culley was concerned. None at all. Impossible. She told herself her depression must just be a case of the holiday blues.

When Elizabeth got to the top of the stairs she saw that the doors to Culley's bedroom and bathroom were both open, and that the lights were on.

Oh great, she thought, he was still up. This was all she needed; the mood she was in tonight, she wasn't sure she could handle another one of those tensely intimate confrontations with Culley.

With her nerves humming like plucked strings,

she took a deep, fortifying breath, directed her eyes straight forward, and prepared to tiptoe unobtrusively by the open doors. Her intentions were good, but the vision framed in the bathroom doorway was just irresistible. She found herself altering course as if pulled by a powerful magnet.

Standing at the sink was a rather emaciated Santa Claus, peering critically at himself in the mirror. When he saw Elizabeth in the doorway he frowned at her and said, "It needs something, don't you think?"

Nine

Realizing that her mouth had been hanging open, Elizabeth closed it and thus managed to gulp the word, "Padding?"

"There is some. A little. Not enough, though, is there? Damn," Culley muttered under his breath, "I should have thought of that. He pivoted and adopted a sideways stance, holding the front of the jacket away from his body. "What do you think? Pillows?"

Elizabeth coughed and said, "Uh, sure. Some pillows would help." She waved her hand and leaned weakly against the door. "Is this . . . why are you . . . what . . . ?"

"Why am I dressed up like this? Because I'm a pushover, and I owed a favor to a friend, that's why. Elizabeth, you've got to help me." He grabbed her by the arm and steered her across the hall to the bedroom. There was panic in his voice. "I've never done anything like this before. I don't know how. Look at me. Who's going to believe me as Santa Claus? Even Wendy wouldn't believe me!"

Elizabeth kept one hand clamped over her mouth to hide her smile and to hold back laughter and the tumult of emotions that were boiling and quivering inside of her. For the moment, all she could do was look at Culley standing there completely enveloped in the voluminous red suit and cascading white beard, his Santa hat prevented from eclipsing his eyes only by the rims of his glasses. And in that moment she knew that the heart doesn't understand the word *impossible*.

"We'll fix it, don't worry," she said, trying to keep laughter and her new realization out of her voice. "Who are you playing Santa Claus for?"

"The kids at Children's Hospital." He shifted and looked away, clearly a little uncomfortable with the confession. "Several years ago, a bunch of us—faculty members and T.A.'s—took some toys over there on Christmas Eve, kind of on the spur of the moment. That started it, I guess. And then how do you stop something like that? It just sort of escalated from there, and now it's a tradition. And a lot of fun. Everybody always has a good time. But the guy who played Santa last year, Mark, my lab assistant, couldn't do it this year, and he asked me if I'd fill in for him. Damn," he muttered under his breath, "I can't believe I let him talk me into this. Caught me in a weak moment." He scowled at Elizabeth, as if she were in some way responsible. "Well, what could I say? His little girl is in some kind of program, and, oh hell." His look turned to one of stark appeal. "What am I going to do?"

"Let's try the pillows," Elizabeth said breathlessly as she pulled two of them out from under the bedspread, hoping that activity would help hide the fact that her heart had turned to mush. She stood with one in her arms, inhaling the scent of Culley from the pillowcase while he poked the other into the front of his suit.

"How do I look?" he asked hopefully when he had rebuckled the wide black belt over the pillow's meager mound.

"Like you're about to give birth to a seven-pound pillow," Elizabeth said, trying to swallow a giggle.

"Here, try the other one. Okay, now we're getting there."

Behind the glasses and whiskers Culley was scowling. "If I move, they're going to fall down my pants legs. This is impossible."

"No it isn't. What we need is some kind of rigging, you know, like a harness. To kind of . . . hold everything in place. Rope, maybe?"

"Not rope," Culley said emphatically. "I'm going to have to be wearing this thing for hours, with little kids climbing on and off my lap. Rope's going to rub."

"Right . . . Oh, wait a minute, I know! Stay right there . . ."

It only took Elizabeth two tries to find the spare bedroom Grace Ward had turned into a sewing room, and only a few minutes more to locate safety pins and the length of muslin she'd noticed when she'd ventured into that room to vacuum and dust.

"Here," she said as she burst back into Culley's room, "I think this'll do fine. Can you take the jacket off for a—Oh!" She stopped as if she'd run into a door, because Culley had already done just that.

It hadn't occurred to her that he wouldn't be wearing anything under the jacket.

He'd taken off the beard and hat, too. All that remained of the Santa suit were the black boots and a pair of too big trousers that clung perilously low on his narrow hips.

She felt shell-shocked, overwhelmed by a barrage of sensory impressions: The way he looked, standing there in the boots and baggy pants, arms folded on his chest, the shadows on his taut belly altering subtly with the rhythms of his breathing. From the neck down, he looked like a young cossack. From the neck up, he looked like a poet. Behind the glasses his eyes were somber, dark and brooding; his hair was long on his neck and forehead, pressed into waves by the weight of the cap and beard and the dampness of his own sweat. . . .

She remembered again the way his body had felt, warm and moist beneath her cheek, the way his heartbeat had sounded, deep and hollow against her ear. She felt his fingers on her chin, smelled his clean, earthy man-smell, heard again his morning-raspy voice whispering her name, and then . . . the sweet, gentle touch of his mouth, and his breath mingling with hers.

Desire was a heavy, pulsing knot in her belly. She pressed her fist against it and felt it burst and pour liquid heat into her legs, making them weak. She felt it surge upward into her chest, altering her breathing, and into her cheeks, making them burn.

"What have you got there?" Culley asked. His voice was husky now, too, as if the air in the room had suddenly grown too thick to breathe. He hadn't missed her reaction to his body, Elizabeth was sure of it. Which made it all the more embarrassing.

Clearing her throat, she advanced with determination. "What I thought we could do is tear some strips of this material, and make straps to go over your shoulders, see? We can pin them to the pillows here and here, and put one in front and one in back, like a sandwich board, you know?" She was speaking rapidly, watching only her hands, refusing to look again into his poet's eyes. ". . . And then, we can pin another set of strips down here and tie them together at the sides. What do you think?"

"Genius," he murmured. She could hear the sound of his breathing.

She turned away with a nervous laugh, preparing to tear the muslin into strips, only to find one hand already full of safety pins. "Oops, here—" she gulped, and turned back just as Culley was reaching out his hand saying, "Here, let me—" Her hand met his bare chest. His wound up clutching her elbow. There was some embarrassed laughter, and a little flurry of apologies.

"Oh—sorry—"

"Sorry!"

"No, that's okay, I didn't mean—"

"What can I—"

"Here, could you—?"

"Yeah, let me take those things. . . ."

Her hands felt loose, out of her control; marionette hands, manipulated by strings. Culley steadied them with his as he took the pins from her, and she felt his touch with every nerve in her body.

I can't do this, she thought, as she tore the muslin into two-inch strips. She couldn't do it without touching him; she'd stick him with a pin for sure.

"Here," she said staunchly, "hold the pillow while I see how long these need to be. . . ."

He held the pillow across his middle with one hand while he handed her the safety pins with the other. With trembling hands she pinned the muslin strips to the pillowcases, right over his smooth pectoral mounds. His skin felt warm against the backs of her fingers. It would take so little, she thought, to lean over and press her mouth against that firm, vibrant muscle, to test its velvety texture with her tongue.

"Thanks," Culley said softly, stirring the damp hair on her forehead with his breath.

Elizabeth murmured something incoherent and kept her eyes on her hands. She felt his chest expand and heard the whisper of his exhalation.

"I just wish the rest of the problem was as easily solved."

Elizabeth's eye's flew upward against her wishes. "What do you mean?"

Barely inches away from her eyes, his mouth curved into a rueful smile. "I still don't have any idea how to be Santa Claus."

"That's easy," Elizabeth said, smiling a little as she resolutely pulled her gaze back to her hands. "You just say Ho Ho Ho a lot and ask everybody if they've been good girls and boys this year. Didn't you ever see Santa Claus when you were a kid?"

"Sure I did. I suppose. I ju.t don't think I have it in me to be . . ." He waved the hand that held the safety pins, frowned and finished, "so uninhibited."

"Oh, you have it in you," Elizabeth chuckled. "Anybody who slides down banisters . . ."

"How did you—ouch!"

"Oh God, I'm sorry—"

"Never mind that, how in the hell did you know about the banister?" He let go of both pillows and pins and caught her by the wrists. And then they were both still, staring at Elizabeth's hands, the fingers splayed wide and pressed flat against Culley's chest.

She's afraid! Culley thought as he felt the tremors coursing through her slender wrists. It suddenly occurred to him to wonder what it was about him that unnerved her—the fact that he was her employer, or the fact that he was a man. It was a new thought, and one he didn't have time to examine at the moment, but either way, it didn't make him happy.

Seeking a way to make the trembling stop, a way to erase that dark, fractured look from her eyes, he said impulsively, "Elizabeth, come with me to the party. You can be my Santa coach. What do you say?"

She'd been staring at him openmouthed. Now she gave her head a little shake and said, "What?"

"Come with me to the party. Everyone brings their families—wives, kids, girlfriends. You'd have fun. And I'd have you to cue me on the Ho Ho Ho's."

"That's . . . Christmas Eve? I'm supposed to take Wendy over to—"

"Bring Wendy along. She'll have a wonderful time too. And afterward, we can drop her off at the Resnicks on the way home. It won't be late. They keep pretty early hours at the hospital."

"I don't know . . . I don't think I have anything to wear."

"Wear anything. You'll look beautiful no matter . . . what . . ."

Culley just sort of ran out of words; Elizabeth's fingers were tracing exquisite patterns over his collarbones. Gazing into her eyes made him feel as if he were standing on a cliff high above the ocean—he could easily succumb to vertigo if he looked too long. He managed to swallow the rock in his throat and whisper, "Elizabeth . . ."

He released her wrists, but somehow, rather than severing the contact between them, it was as if he'd released a brake. Her hands slid upward to his shoulders, and then to his neck. His hands moved along her arms, pushing the sleeves of her sweatshirt out of the way, his thumbs stroking circles on the inner bends of her elbows. . . . Then up and over the bunched-up fabric, fighting the urge to tear it off her, fighting for restraint, fighting for control; finding soft skin again, fingers probing greedily inside the neck of her sweatshirt, hungry for the silkiness, and all the varied textures of her.

Her neck was so slender, so strong and vital in his hands—as she was. He lowered his head and felt her small hands, those delicate fingers, weave themselves through the hair on the back of his neck. He closed his eyes and felt the sweet stirring of her breath on his lips. He growled something—it may have been an oath or a prayer, it may have been her name—and cradling her head in his two hands, sliding his fingers into the flame-gold masses of her hair, claimed her mouth with his.

It was a hungry kiss. No tender awakening, no tentative exploration, no sensuous melding, but a bruising explosion of passions held back too long. His mouth covered hers; hers blossomed inside his, both fighting and yielding, lifting, opening, demanding, giving. Culley poured himself into her, possessing her with his tongue as he could not with his body. And she responded to him like a thirsty wanderer to a cooling spring, drinking him in and surging to vibrant, pulsing life under his mouth and hands.

He could feel surrender in the weight of her head in his hands, taste it in the warm, sweet essence of her mouth, hear it in the low wordless sounds she made as she strained against him. The pillow caught between their bodies was a frustration to them both; Culley finally had to tear his mouth from hers and, muttering curses under his breath, haul the thing over his head and toss it away. Santa Claus was forgotten, Christmas parties were forgotten, his history and hers . . . forgotten. He couldn't think why he hadn't done this weeks ago. His conscience, his scruples, even his patience seemed foolish to him now.

He reached for her, slipping his hands under the bottom of her shirt, molding her soft, creamy flesh, feeling it heat and tremble in his hands. He felt her palms press against his back, her fingers splay and dig deep into his muscles, holding him with passion's unconscious strength. Her eyes looked glazed; her mouth was bruised and wet from his kiss.

Culley felt as if he were going to explode; the heat in his loins was unbearable. Under her sweatshirt his hands were discovering Elizabeth's small, round breasts, the fact that she wasn't wearing a bra. Her nipples were hard as pebbles against his palms. There was no way, he thought, that he was going to be able to let her go back to her own chaste bed tonight. Her breasts were swelling, lifting into his hands. He wanted—needed!—to cover their tender tips with his mouth and draw them deep . . . deep, until she moaned and gasped, mindless with pleasure. He wanted her satin skin next to his, her body writhing under his, her loins cradling his, her low cries mingling with his as he immersed himself in her sweet, hot depths.

Elizabeth sighed. Her lashes drifted down. She

leaned into his hands, wordlessly pleading. Culley slipped his hands around to her sides and began slowly to lift them, drawing her shirt upward. Her breathing accelerated, her ribcage expanded, her skin roughened with shivers of excitement.

And then they heard a sound that brought them both to a trembling, heart-thumping halt:

"What doin', Mom?"

Elizabeth breathed, "Oh . . . God," and let her head fall against Culley's chest. Every parent's nightmare. . . .

Culley was silent, not even swearing. She could feel the movement of his throat as he swallowed repeatedly, feel the heavy hammering of his heart against her cheek. He had let his hands slide back to her waist, but hadn't let go of her yet. She held on to his forearms, feeling the tight adrenaline tremors deep in his muscles, the warmth of his hands on her skin. . . . She wanted to cry.

"Elizabeth . . ."

She sighed and lifted her head, willing strength into muscles grown weak as a newborn kitten's. Wendy was standing in the doorway, shaky and squinting, her security blanket a forlorn bundle under one arm. "Oh, baby . . ." Elizabeth whispered, and moved to her on legs that felt like noodles, missing the strong support of Culley's arms as she'd miss one of her own limbs.

"What doin', Mommy?" Wendy quavered once more, but Elizabeth knew she wasn't really awake. She wouldn't remember any of this in the morning. It gave her small comfort.

Throwing Culley a look of stark appeal, she calmly picked up her daughter and carried her back to her bed. She kissed and soothed her and tucked her in with a not too subtle warning that Santa Claus doesn't bring toys to little girls who won't stay in their own beds at night. And then she went out and shut the door and leaned against it, shuddering.

"What are we going to do about this?" Culley asked quietly. He was standing in her bedroom doorway, one hand braced high on the doorframe.

Elizabeth gave a silent, painful laugh and turned away from him, reaching up to latch the hook and eye on Wendy's door. Locking the barn door . . . "You asked me that once before, remember?"

"Elizabeth . . ." She felt him move close to her, felt him slip his hand under her hair and cradle the back of her neck, his touch both tender and sensuous. It sent shivers of sensation through her body, making her want to move against his hand like a cat being petted. Fighting the desire made her jaws ache.

"Elizabeth, we have to deal with this."

"*Deal* with this?" All at once she felt testy, even angry. "I don't even know what it is I'm dealing with!" His hand tightened on her nape in mute sympathy, and that gentle pressure became the most exquisite of tortures, an ache she felt in her throat, in her ears, behind her eyes, and under her cheekbones. If only she could arch and bow sinuously beneath his hand, and then turn smiling into his embrace, it would be the most exquisite of pleasures, instead. . . . "I'm confused," she whispered, in painful understatement.

"I know," Culley said softly. "I know. I understand."

But Elizabeth was fairly certain he didn't understand at all. It's *you,* she wanted to scream at him. *You* confuse me! I don't know how you feel about me! I don't know what you want from me! I don't know what I'm supposed to be to you!

But she just didn't have the self-confidence and courage to tell him how she felt, and to demand the same honesty from him in return.

It was different in his arms. In his arms, with his hands caressing her body and his mouth possessing hers, her response was instinctive, mindless . . . woman to man. She could give without reservation and demand without shyness. The only voices she heard were those of passion, and the questions were simple: Do you want this . . . do you desire me . . . am I giving you pleasure? And the answers were even simpler, and impossible to hide: Yes . . . yes . . . yes!

But like this, facing him, talking to him, meeting his eyes, he was . . . Culley—no, Dr. Ward!—and she was just his housekeeper—she was nobody! How could she possibly tell him she'd fallen in love with him? Especially since she had no business falling in love with anybody. . . .

"I know you're confused . . . and I'm sorry," Culley said roughly, letting his hand fall away from her neck. She bowed her head and wished it back again with every fiber of her being. He raked his fingers through his hair, hesitated, then started down the hall to his room. Halfway there he paused to look back. "Elizabeth? Come to the hospital with me anyway. Please? I really would like to have you there."

There was so much in his voice that she didn't dare believe in. It was all she could manage to nod and choke out the word, "Sure."

Christmas, she thought bitterly, watching his bedroom door close. The loneliest time of the year.

The next few days fell back into the pattern of the previous weeks. Elizabeth bought a Christmas tree, which she and Wendy decorated with ornaments she found in the closet under the stairs. She put candles in brass candlesticks on the mantel in the living room, and a crèche on the hall table. She looped artificial evergreen garlands down the banister and tied a huge red bow on the newel post. She and Wendy cut armloads of juniper, pine, and holly, and heavy clusters of the red pyracantha berries that grew along the walls of the estate, and strewed them all over the house, bringing the smell of Christmas indoors. She bought a sprig of mistletoe from some Cub Scouts who were selling it in front of the supermarket, and after a great deal of consideration, hung it in the library doorway. It seemed safest there.

While she was hanging the mistletoe, standing on a chair to hammer a tack into the wooden doorframe, she could almost . . . *almost* hear voices in the room behind her, happy voices, children's voices, singing and laughing . . . If she closed her eyes she would see them, shining eyes and rosy cheeks amidst the litter of wrapping paper, cups of eggnog and spiced cider . . . and Culley, coming to swing her down from the chair, whirl her into his arms and kiss her until she grew dizzy, while the children laughed and giggled at the silliness of their parents. . . .

Meanwhile, Culley worked late. She saw him only in the mornings with Wendy as chaperone.

She bought him a present, though, finally, and wrapped it and put it under the tree. She baked a mince pie and a pumpkin pie, and made fudge, and she and Wendy cut out and decorated Christmas cookies. She bought a small goose to roast for Culley's Christmas dinner.

Two days before Christmas, while Wendy was napping, she uncovered the sewing machine in the spare bedroom and sewed the muslin straps onto the pillows for Culley to wear under his Santa suit. Then she searched through her closet and finally pulled out a dress she'd last worn to a high school dance. It was dark green, and had a tulip-shaped taffeta skirt and a fitted velveteen bodice with bare shoulders and a sweetheart neckline. It was ten years out of style, but it did look vaguely Christmasy, and when she tried it on, it still fit her. She thought it would do for the party at the hospital, although she couldn't help but wish she could afford to buy something new and wonderful, maybe a slinky little black number . . . something expensive and glamorous. Something that would knock Culley's eyes out.

• • •

The day before Christmas, Culley worked at the lab until noon and then went over to the hospital to help with the decorations for the party. He took the Santa suit with him and put it in the staff lounge to change into later that evening, since he couldn't very well wear it in the car with Elizabeth and Wendy.

He got home with barely time to shower and change clothes. Wendy ran to meet him, already dressed for the party, looking like an angel in a white dress with red velvet ribbons woven through its ruffles, red tights, black patent leather shoes and a red velvet ribbon in her hair.

"Daddy's home!" she crowed with uninhibited delight, making Culley feel guilty about all the times lately when he'd come home after she'd gone to bed.

"Hi, squirt," he said gruffly, reaching out to tweak a ruffle. "You look pretty tonight. All ready to go to the party?"

Wendy nodded emphatically. "Goin' to see Santa Claus!"

Culley winced. "You are?"

"Yeah. I'm a *good* girl."

"You sure are," Culley murmured. Something strange was happening to his chest. It felt . . . crowded. "You're a sweetheart, you know that?"

Wendy beamed. "I'm a *sweetheart!*"

"Oh—hi." Elizabeth's voice floated down to him from upstairs. "I didn't hear you come in. Is Wendy—"

"She's right here." Culley stood up very slowly and watched her come down the stairs. She was wearing a dress, a short, cocktail-type dress in rich dark green that left her legs and most of her chest and shoulders bare. In somewhat of a daze, it occurred to Culley that it was the first time he'd ever seen her legs.

"Is this all right?" Elizabeth asked uncertainly, pausing on the bottom step. One slender white hand rested on the newel post, as if she needed that support. Red-gold curls stirred softly on her shoulders, licking her creamy skin like flames.

"You look—" Culley cleared his throat and amended hoarsely, "—fine." Tearing his eyes reluctantly away from her, he muttered, "Wait right there a minute—" and picked up his briefcase. He laid it on the hall table, twirled the combination lock with fingers that weren't quite steady, opened it and took out two small oblong packages. One was wrapped in red foil with gold poinsettias on it; the other had pictures of Snoopy in a Santa hat. "Here," he said gruffly, handing the foil-wrapped package to Elizabeth, "this is for you. I was going to wait until later, but . . . I thought—well, just go ahead, open it."

Her eyes clung to his, dark and gray as a winter sky. "This is . . . for me?"

"Go on, open it."

She did, looking up at him from time to time, as if she were afraid he might vanish in a puff of smoke. Culley found that his heart was beating fast and hard; he felt as if he were eleven years old again, trying to get up enough nerve to kiss Amy Weismuller in the old arbor swing.

"Oh . . ." It was a spontaneous cry of pure delight, and it warmed Culley's insides like a swallow of aged brandy. "Oh, it's . . . just beautiful."

"Wanna see, Mommy!"

Elizabeth lifted the gold locket from its box and held it to the light.

"I was going to give it to you tomorrow, but I thought it might look nice with what you're wearing," Culley said uncomfortably. "If you'd like, I can . . . uh." She handed the necklace to him without a word, her eyes shining so that he could almost see himself reflected in their depths, and turned, lifting her hair and tilting her head to bare her slender neck. The brandy warmth in Culley's chest spread like liquid fire through his veins.

As he struggled with the tiny fastener, he whispered to Elizabeth, "I have one for Wendy, too, only smaller. I didn't know whether I should give it to her now, or . . . you know, let Santa do it?"

"Give it to her now," Elizabeth whispered back, smiling. "She understands about giving presents. She has something for you too."

Culley nodded and, taking the Snoopy present from under his arm, dropped to one knee in front of Wendy. "Merry Christmas, squirt. This is for you."

Wendy tore off the wrappings in a suspenseful hush, and refused help opening the box with an emphatic, "I do it!" Only a moment later, though, she thrust the box at Culley and demanded, "Daddy, help it."

Her face lit up like a Christmas tree when she saw the locket. "Like Mommy's!" she cried, so excited she could barely stand still long enough for Culley to fasten it around her neck.

"See," he told her, demonstrating, "you can open it up, like this. Then you can put pictures inside. You could put your mommy's picture in there."

Wendy nodded. "And Daddy's."

Elizabeth made a strangled sound. "Uh, Wendy, why don't you go get Culley his present. Remember where you put it, under the Christmas tree?"

Wendy went dashing off into the living room. Culley looked up at Elizabeth, but she was steadfastly avoiding his eyes. In a moment Wendy was back with a small cube-shaped, clumsily wrapped box, which she shoved into Culley's hands. Planting her tongue self-consciously in her cheek, she slipped between Culley's knees and leaned against his chest while he opened his present.

"It's a cup," Wendy announced, an instant or so too soon.

And so it was. A plastic cup with a picture of Solar the Antarian and his beloved Princess Kerissa on it. Culley looked up at Elizabeth and found her looking at him now with laughter-flushed cheeks and shining eyes.

"She picked it out all by herself," she murmured. "Didn't you, Wendy?"

Wendy nodded and squirmed shyly. Culley hugged her and tweaked her nose. "It's the best cup I ever got. Thanks a lot, squirt." His voice was scratchy, and he had that crowded feeling in his chest again. He coughed and stood up. "Well. I guess I'd better go get showered. Wouldn't do for me to be late, would it?"

He headed up the stairs pretty quickly. Not, he told himself, that he was the macho sort who couldn't let his emotions show. He was just afraid Wendy wouldn't understand.

Culley could move pretty efficiently when he needed to. Even with a small side trip to his office in the attic, in fifteen minutes he was back downstairs with his composure intact, wearing a jacket and tie.

Elizabeth and Wendy were waiting for him in the living room, watching a Hanna-Barbera Christmas cartoon on television. She must have heard him on the stairs, because when he walked in, she was just tying the strings of Wendy's Red Riding Hood cape under her chin.

"We're all ready," she said, smiling up at him. She stood up and reached for the coat that lay on the arm of the couch. Culley recognized it—it was the one she'd been wearing that first night, when she'd knocked on his front door and he'd mistaken her for a trick-or-treater. It seemed like a year ago.

"Don't put that on." He reached quickly to stay her hand. When she turned to him, her mouth just opening to form a question, he touched her shoulder and murmured, "Here, try this instead."

She uttered one soft gasp as the velvet cloak settled around her shoulders. Her startled eyes flew to his, and one hand fluttered up to touch the rich green folds.

"There," he growled as he pulled the hood up to frame her fire-bright hair. "That's better. What do you think?"

Elizabeth whispered, "I don't know what to think. It's . . . it's beautiful." Her hand was stroking the thick dark velvet. She seemed stunned.

Just then Wendy, who had been staring at her mother in silent awe, reached out to touch the cloak with one chubby finger, and whispered, "Princess."

Elizabeth burst into nervous laughter. "Oh, baby."

"It was my grandmother's," Culley lied glibly, offering her his arm. "I don't think she'd mind if you wore it. Now, if you're ready—"

"Princess," Wendy said with more confidence, patting the shimmering velvet material. She turned sparkling pixie eyes to Culley. "Princess Kiss—"

"Oh, *I* know why she's saying that," Elizabeth said in an artificially bright voice, catching her daughter's hand. "She's probably thinking about that dark green cloak Princess Kerissa wears in *Solar's Revenge*. It did look something like this one, remember?"

"No," Culley muttered. "I didn't see it."

"I can't believe you never saw *Solar's Revenge*," Elizabeth said with a laugh, taking his arm. "It was just on cable. That's where Wendy saw it."

"I can't believe you let her watch a movie like that," Culley said darkly as they went out the door.

Elizabeth gave him a look he couldn't figure out. "How do you know what kind of movie it is," she said softly, showing that elusive dimple of hers, "if you've never seen it?"

"Hmm," Culley growled. He didn't have an answer for that one.

Ten

Elizabeth went through the rest of the evening in a daze. She was in such a muddle of emotions she didn't know what she was saying or doing. She'd been so depressed, looking forward to this evening with Culley, but dreading it too; dreading being with him, and yet *not* with him; dreading the moment when she'd have to drop Wendy off with the Resnicks and face Christmas all alone. . . .

But from the moment she'd come down the stairs to see that look on Culley's face . . . like a blind man restored to sight and witnessing his first sunrise . . . she'd felt as if she'd fallen into a kaleidoscope. Everything around her seemed to be in indecipherable fragments; and just when she started to make sense of anything, the pattern shifted and became another confusing jumble.

He'd made her feel beautiful . . . special . . . important . . . cherished. As he'd done so many times before, beginning on that Halloween night when he'd covered her and Wendy with his own bedspread and tiptoed quietly away, leaving two strangers asleep in his bed. And at those times he'd almost made her believe she might be good enough for him after all, that the fact that she was his little nobody of a housekeeper didn't matter. But then he'd follow that up by distancing himself from her, avoiding her, acting as if nothing special or important or beautiful had ever happened between them, until now she felt she didn't dare allow herself to believe it was real anymore.

And yet . . . the cloak was real. She felt its weight on her shoulders, felt its warmth enveloping her body. Princess Kerissa's cloak, which Elizabeth had first seen on a twenty-foot movie screen . . . and which she'd last seen draped on a mannequin in Culley's attic office. Why had he given it to her? What did it *mean*?

There was only one way she was ever going to find out, she realized. Sooner or later she was going to have to get up enough courage to ask the only one who knew the answer. She'd have to ask Culley.

Tonight, she said to herself. After the party. After they'd dropped Wendy off at the Resnicks. They would be alone, and it was Christmas Eve. She'd ask him tonight.

Stores were still open, and traffic was heavy with last minute Christmas shoppers, so they were late getting to the hospital. By the time Culley found a parking place and took care of Elizabeth's and Wendy's cloaks and found his way through the maze of corridors to the cafeteria, Marge, the auxiliary lady who was coordinating the party, had been looking for him in a state of panic.

"Dr. Ward, where in the *world*—" The conspirator's whisper with which Marge greeted him changed to a lilting song when she saw Wendy clinging to Elizabeth's hand: "—We've been wor-ried about yoo-ou!" Taking his arm in a schoolteacher's hold, she hustled him toward the staff lounge, whispering out of the side of her mouth. "Everything's ready for your grand entrance, but we'll stall a few more minutes to give you time to change. I think everything's in here. Costume . . . toy sack . . . do you need anything else?"

"No," Culley said, "I don't think so." He was looking back over his shoulder at Elizabeth and Wendy. They looked lost.

"Go on, I'll see to your friend and the little one," Marge said, patting his shoulder in a grandmotherly way. "*You* go get dressed!"

Elizabeth found his eyes and smiled. Culley nodded and went into the lounge.

"Remember," Marge whispered as she was leaving, "don't come out until you hear everybody singing 'Jingle Bells.' "

"Right," Culley said to the closing door. He wished he could have asked Elizabeth to come in and help him. Not that he needed help with the costume, he just wanted her near, wanted to see that dimple of hers, and to hear her voice teasing him about the Ho Ho Ho's.

While he was changing into the Santa suit he tried saying "Ho Ho Ho," a few times in a big jolly voice. He felt like an idiot. "It's easy," Elizabeth had told him, laughing.

"Easy for *you* to say," he muttered under his breath. Which was more than he could say about a lot of other things. His frustration level where Elizabeth was concerned was approaching combustion point.

He'd surprised himself tonight, giving Elizabeth the cloak. He hadn't known he was going to do that, not right then, anyway. He realized that it amounted to a statement, an admission, as much to himself as to her. He'd only known her a couple of months, but Culley made up his mind pretty quickly about these things. He'd only known Shannon a couple of weeks before he'd realized he loved her. . . .

"Dashing through the snow . . . in a one-horse open sleigh. . . ."

Oh Lord, Culley thought, sending up one last fervent plea for deliverance. There it was. Time for his grand entrance. Taking a last deep breath, he opened the door.

"Ho Ho Ho! Merr-ry Christmas!"

When Elizabeth saw Culley come through the door with his huge bag of toys, she thought her heart would leap through the walls of her chest. She could only gaze at him through a besotted shimmer.

He's so wonderful . . . he's the most wonderful, beautiful Santa Claus in the world. . . .

"Ho Ho Ho!" Culley rumbled, scooping Wendy up in his arms. "And how are you, Wendy? Have you been a good girl?"

Wendy leaned back, stared at him for a moment, then pointed and said clearly, "Daddy's glasses!"

Elizabeth's stomach did a flip-flop. Culley's eyes flew to hers, and she saw panic in them. She lifted her shoulders helplessly; he was on his own now.

"Do you wear glasses?" a child whose head was completely bald asked shyly.

"Hey—I never heard of no Santa Claus with glasses," said a sullen-looking older boy with a cast on one arm and bruises on his face and neck—from an accident, Elizabeth supposed, or a severe beating.

"Hey," Culley boomed, reaching out one gloved hand to draw the boy against his side, "don't you know Old Santa's eyes get tired, reading all your letters? All those Christmas lists? And don't forget, he has to check 'em twice!" A few of the children giggled. "Hey, I know what I'm gonna do—" Scooping up a little girl in Winnie-the-Pooh slippers, Culley settled himself in a chair. "I'm gonna tell you a story. Who wants to hear a story?"

The children began to move closer. Culley arranged Wendy on one knee and the Pooh slippers on the other. The child with no hair leaned against his side and asked, "What kind of story?"

"Uh . . . well, let's see. You've heard all the ones

about Rudolph, I suppose, haven't you? And Frosty? Saw those on television, I'll bet." There was a chorus of enthusiastic agreement. But nearly all of the children had gathered around Culley now, and were making themselves comfortable at his feet. Over their heads, Culley's eyes searched for and found Elizabeth's.

"This is a new story," he said, holding on to her eyes as if his words were for her alone. "And it's a very old story. It's about a lonely, cranky wizard who lived all alone in a great big castle. Until one day—"

"Why was he cranky?" the child with no hair interrupted.

"Why? Because he didn't have a heart, that's why. You see . . ." Culley's voice was a low rumble that Elizabeth felt all through her insides, like a cat's purr. "A long time ago, the wizard's heart had gotten broken, so he'd put it away in a cupboard where it would be safe. So he wouldn't have to worry about it getting broken again. And he lived all alone, getting crankier by the day, until one day, a beautiful lost princess came to the castle and knocked on the door. Now, this princess had a little girl—"

"Like me?" the child with no hair asked.

Culley looked at the child in some surprise, and then put his arm around her and hugged her. "Yeah," he said in a voice that had suddenly become rusty, "just like you . . ."

He looked at Elizabeth. When he saw her lift a hand and secretly wipe her eyes, his own emotions nearly swamped him and all but scuttled his story. No doubt about it, he thought, shaken. He loved her. And he loved the yellow-haired pixie sitting on his knee too.

And he knew there was a pretty good chance they might love him back.

". . . And so the wizard gave his heart to the princess and the little girl, and they all lived happily ever after. . . ."

The trouble was, Culley thought later as he was changing back into his own clothes—and the real world—that while he knew *he* was ready for a real relationship, he didn't think Elizabeth was. In spite of her obvious attraction to him, he sensed a reserve in her—some sort of conflict. Something was holding her back. Maybe it was just her natural grieving process, and maybe not, but he was afraid she was never going to get over it if she kept holding it all inside. Damn it, he thought, she just needed to *talk* to someone—preferably him.

Culley was a patient man. He had to be, to be able to devote a good part of his life to watching isotopes break down—the nuclear age equivalent of watching sequoia trees grow. But dammit, he thought, life was too short for this. He'd been alone long enough. There was a limit to his patience. Communication, he told himself; that was the key. He had to force the issue, find some way to get Elizabeth to talk about herself.

Tonight, he promised himself. They'd be together tonight. Alone. It was Christmas Eve. He'd talk to her tonight.

"Well," Elizabeth said as the front door clicked softly, shutting them in with the warm smells of juniper and spices, "that was easy."

Her back was toward him as she said it, but Culley could see her face in the mirror over the hall table, still framed in the graceful drape of the cloak's hood. Even in the golden light of the wall sconces it looked pale and strained.

Oh, Elizabeth . . . he thought; but all he said was, "What was easy?"

"Leaving Wendy. I really expected a bigger fuss, but she was just so tired—half asleep, really. I don't think she knew what was going on, do you?"

Culley murmured something in agreement. Elizabeth glanced up as she slipped the hood back, meeting his eyes in the mirror. He almost winced at the pain in them.

"She had so much fun at the hospital," she went on, flashing him a bright, plastic smile, one that didn't show her dimple. "We both did. I'm so glad you asked us to go. I think everyone had a good time, don't you?" Her voice escalated as she moved away from him, chattering on and on. "All the children . . . I really think Wendy's made a new friend. Did you see how she and that little girl with the Winnie-the-Pooh slippers were hitting it off? I think her name was Angie. . . ."

Dammit, Elizabeth! They'd already had this conversation in the car. What Culley really wanted to do was take her by the shoulders and shake her until all that reserve broke loose, to shout at her that it was *okay* to hurt, and okay to show it, too. Talk to me, dammit, talk to me!

". . . And I thought you were a great Santa. Just great. The Ho Ho Ho's were perfect, and the way you handled that business about the glasses—that was great, just like a pro. And the story . . ."

Culley reached for her to help her off with the cloak, but she slipped out of it herself and knelt down to plug in the Christmas tree, deftly avoiding his touch.

"What did you think of my story?" Culley asked softly.

"Oh—I thought it was cute. Really cute." Pastel light from the Christmas tree flooded the room. Elizabeth stood up, dusting her hands, and flashing him another bright smile. "All kids love stories. That was a stroke of genius, you know—oops!" She gave a self-conscious giggle and touched her lips with her fingertips. "Well, what else, right?"

He didn't smile. Her fingers shifted nervously to the gold locket at the base of her throat. Culley's eyes followed. Her gaze snagged on his and he saw it darken. And he thought, You don't hide your feelings as well as you'd like to, Elizabeth, your eyes talk too much. . . .

Turning from him, she reached for the box of fireplace matches on the mantel. He caught her arm and took them from her.

"Hey," he said softly, "it's Christmas Eve. You're off duty. I'll do that."

She coughed and fidgeted uncertainly, then brightened. "Would you like some eggnog? I made some earlier this afternoon. It's in the refrigerator. I'll just go—"

"Elizabeth." Culley looked up from laying the fire and shook his head. "Just . . . turn on your Out of Service light, will you? Sit down. Relax."

Already halfway across the room, she paused, thought for a moment, and then said, "Is it okay if I go and get *myself* some eggnog?"

Culley laughed. "By all means."

In a few minutes she was back with a crystal pitcher full of eggnog and two old-fashioned glasses on a tray.

"Since I was already up, I thought I might as well bring you some," she murmured as she poured eggnog into the glasses. Through the gossamer curtain of her hair, Culley caught a glimpse of her dimple.

She seemed more relaxed, less edgy. As he took the glass she handed him Culley thought sardonically that it was probably being away from him for awhile that had calmed her down.

"Hmm," he said, taking a sip of eggnog, "needs something. Isn't it supposed to have brandy or something in it?"

"Rum, I think. There wasn't any." Elizabeth's eyes flicked towards the Christmas tree. "Um . . . I think you should open your present."

"Now? Not Christmas morning?"

"Better now, I think. Besides, it's the only one left."

She brought the package to him and stood self-consciously by, watching him, sipping her eggnog while he opened it.

It was a bottle of cognac. A very large bottle of what Culley happened to know was very fine, very expensive cognac. He knew it would have taken a good-sized chunk out of Elizabeth's tiny salary.

"I didn't know what to get you," she said uncertainly. "I got the idea from that beautiful crystal decanter and snifters in the cabinet in the library. It just seemed to . . . I don't know . . ." She made a vague motion with her hand, taking in him and the room in all its high-ceilinged elegance, then gave a throaty little laugh and lowered her voice an octave. "You know, Victorian gentlemen retiring to the library after dinner for brandy and cigars. . . ."

Good heavens! Culley thought, is that how she sees me? *As a Victorian gentleman?* And then it occurred to him that lately he'd been behaving a lot like one—starched, inhibited, righteous and hypocritical. As a matter of fact, since Elizabeth had moved into his house, he'd been squelching quite a few of his normal, healthy twentieth-century male impulses.

". . . Anyway, I thought maybe you could put some in your eggnog. If you wanted to."

"It'd be a shame to waste this on eggnog," Culley muttered reverently, breaking the seal on the bottle. "I mean, this is good stuff. Something like this . . ." He inhaled the brandy's heady aroma and sighed. "This . . . needs to be savored, with all the senses." And then he happened to glance at Elizabeth and he caught that flushed, shining look she got sometimes, and he thought, Who needs brandy?

"Oh!" she cried, setting her eggnog glass down on the coffee table, looking both pleased and uncertain. "You mean you'd like to—wait a minute, I'll go and get the snifters!"

Culley plunked the bottle of cognac down beside

her glass. "Elizabeth, wait—for God's sake—I can do that!"

They both got to the library doorway at the same time.

"Culley, please, it's no trouble—"

"Elizabeth." He put his hands on the upper part of her arms and turned her to face him. Her mouth opened, closed, then opened again. "Elizabeth," he ground out before she could start chattering again, "will you cut it out? I don't expect you to wait on me hand and foot! I'm not a Victorian." He paused, looking down at the place where the dark green velvet of her dress met the creamy white silk of her skin. "And incidentally, right now I don't feel much like a gentleman, either."

He saw her throat move. In a small, constricted voice she said, "But . . . you shouldn't be waiting on me. I'm your—"

Culley's breath hissed between his teeth as his hand closed over her mouth, cutting off the word. "Elizabeth, I swear, if you say that one more time, I'll—" He raised his eyes heavenward in total exasperation. And halted in midsigh. Chuckling softly with satisfaction, he brought his eyes back to Elizabeth's. "I'll . . . kiss you."

Her eyes stared back at him over his hand . . . wide, luminous, transparent. When he eased his hand away from her mouth she whispered, "What?"

"I'm going to kiss you," Culley said, his lips curving in a smile. "There are some old-fashioned customs I don't mind honoring."

Her startled gaze flicked upward; her mouth formed a soft, pink O. Culley's fingers found the velvety place under her chin and gently lifted. He lowered his head slowly, catching the sharp intake of her breath, feeling the slight tensing in her muscles. He covered her mouth slowly, feeling it soften and then blossom to fullness under his, feeling her lips move, adjusting to the shape of his. He began to taste her with his tongue, exploring her textures, savoring her, as he would a fine brandy, with all his senses. . . .

And he felt the trembling begin. He felt it in her mouth, first, and then in the depths of her body, and pulling back a little, looked down into her face. Her eyes were closed, and there were stress marks between them. Drawing his thumb across her moisture-glazed lips, he whispered, "What's the matter?"

The stress marks deepened. "Nothing." But he could feel the battle in her, the resistance, the hunger and the yearning.

Elizabeth, talk to me!

With his hand he felt the tight little convulsion of her swallow. "I don't—I want—"

"Yes," he encouraged, "tell me."

"I want . . . you to kiss me."

His heart surged inside his chest, forcing a small gust of laughter from him. "Oh, I will," he said huskily, "but first, there's something I have to tell you."

"What?" The question was hushed, expectant.

Culley smiled into her eyes, then lowered his head and softly whispered, "You're fired."

That knocked her off balance, as he'd figured it would. As she deflated with an exhalation of pure shock he chuckled and pulled her into his arms.

"I'll hire you back, of course—right after Christmas. But Elizabeth—" He gripped her arms and held her away from him again, far enough, at least, to look into her eyes. "Dammit, Elizabeth, just for once—will you please forget about being my housekeeper? Tonight you're nobody's housekeeper. You're just . . . a warm, beautiful woman, who . . ." he finished in a low, rough voice, "I want very much to be with."

She looked at him as if he'd lost his mind. Since she didn't seem to have anything to say, and he didn't either, he did what both of them seemed to want more than talking anyway. He kissed her.

He kissed her and went on kissing her, stroking,

tasting, deliciously exploring every inch of her mouth, inside and out . . . until finally she had to pull away, gasping . . . and cling to him, trembling. . . .

"Culley—" Her breath was hot and moist against his shirt front.

"Yes . . ." he soothed, gently kneading her shoulders, letting the sensitive pads of his fingers revel in the luxury of her skin. "What is it? Tell me. . . ."

"Culley, I think . . . I *need* you," she whispered finally, telling him only what he already knew.

"Nothing wrong with that," he said gruffly.

"But . . ." He felt her shoulders shift under his hands as she pressed herself against him, burying her face deeper into the hollow of his throat. "I don't know . . . I feel . . . I think I'm . . scared."

Culley's heart trembled within him. He felt as if he were coaxing a wild bird into his hand . . . and she was close, so close. "I know," he murmured, touching the words tenderly to the top of her head. "But you don't have to be." He cupped the back of her head in his hand, softly stroked her hair and then applied a firm but gentle pressure so that she was obliged to leave the sanctuary of his shirt front and look at him. "Elizabeth, nothing is going to happen that you don't want to happen."

She clung to his eyes so avidly, he could see she was trying hard to believe him. "Culley, I have to ask you something."

"Anything. Ask me."

She closed her eyes and cleared her throat, as if preparing herself for an ordeal. "What did you mean tonight?" Her fingertips touched the gold locket at her throat, like a butterfly alighting on a flower. "Giving me this, and then the story?"

"Good God." Culley's voice was soft with wonder. "Elizabeth, don't you know?"

Hungry eyes searched his, probing to the depths of his soul. At last, wonderingly, as if she still couldn't believe it, she whispered, "You're the wizard. . . ."

". . . And you are the princess." Culley put his hand over hers, covering both it and the locket, holding them next to her skin. "And . . . I've given you my heart."

I've given you my heart.

So breathtakingly simple, Elizabeth thought. So impossibly romantic, so beautifully . . . Culley.

And because he was so beautiful to her, the look in his eyes as simple and straightforward as his words, she couldn't bear to look at him any longer. The honesty of his emotions overwhelmed her. She'd thought his messages mixed, but looking back on it, she realized that his messages had been clear enough, if only she'd dared to read them. He'd been keeping his distance from her because he thought *she* needed it, giving her time to heal her own broken heart, giving her time to get over her grief. *Grief!* Dear God, she thought, what would he think of her if he knew the truth?

Bubbles of ironic laughter twisted painfully through her chest, emerging in a small, desperate sob as she closed her eyes and lifted her arms blindly to his neck. Culley's response was a wordless exclamation, almost a growl; she could feel it rumbling through his chest as his arms tightened around her.

And now it was her own emotions that overwhelmed her. She felt swamped by him, steeped in the heat of his body . . . and it wasn't nearly enough! Her body ached with emptiness; she wanted him to fill it. She wanted to take him into herself, surround him, be surrounded by him, immersed in him, until she couldn't tell where she left off and he began. . . .

His fingers found her zipper and pulled it down. His hands pulled the halves of her dress aside and covered her flesh greedily, his palms stroking her sides, fingers kneading her back, thumbs outlining the delicate undercurve of her breasts. And then, holding her like that his hands suddenly tightened. "Elizabeth—" he said thickly, separating her from him and bowing his head so that his forehead touched hers, "in case there's any doubt in your mind, I want to make love to you. I want you in my bed tonight, all night . . . but—" his voice grew husky . . . guttural, "—I don't want to pressure you. I don't want you to do anything you're not ready for . . . do you understand?"

Elizabeth shook her head, not because she didn't understand, but because she didn't want to talk, or think, or remember. She didn't want to feel any more guilt, or anger, or fear. She only wanted to feel *Culley*, his hands and mouth touching her, stroking her to mindless, all-consuming passion; his body heavy on hers, his strength and power filling her. . . .

"I can stop if you want me to," Culley whispered. "You go to your bed . . . and I'll go to mine."

Elizabeth stared at him, dumb with desire. Culley's hands moved slowly on her sides, stroking shivers into her skin, raising her nipples to tender erection, making the brush of fabric across them an intolerable torture. She wanted his mouth there instead, soothing with sweet, liquid warmth. . . .

Finally, because he seemed to need the reassurance, she summoned all her remaining self-control and said clearly and distinctly, "That would be ridiculous."

His chuckle was ragged and gentle. Lowering his head a little further, he let his laughter shiver across her parted lips. "Yeah, I guess it would . . ." His tongue slid over her lips, glazing them with moisture, then slipped between them in a slow, sensuous, deliberately evocative penetration. Her bones melted.

She should have known he would carry her up the stairs. What she couldn't have anticipated was that she would feel so relaxed . . . weightless . . . steeped in a kind of sensual lethargy that was like floating in a tub of warm water. All of her anxieties and inhibitions simply . . . drifted away. She arched into his hands while he undressed her, responding to his touch with an almost feline pleasure, then lay unashamedly naked in the soft light of a bedside lamp and watched him undress, making no effort to disguise her hunger. When he came to her she reached for him, letting her hands, her eyes, her mouth tell him without words how beautiful she found his body, how much she wanted him.

Culley wondered how he'd ever managed to wait so long. Lying there with her hair spreading like filaments of fire across his bed, her lush and slender body pale against his sheets, she seemed to him all beauty, all softness. And yet, all woman too, and as wanton and unreserved in her response to him as he could ever have dreamed she might be. Her eyes, heavy-lidded and slumberous; her mouth, swollen and moist from his kisses; her skin, suffused with the rosy glow of passion; her breasts, small, firm, their perfection marred slightly by the faint pink lines that in Culley's eyes only made them more beautiful.

He leaned over her, bracing his hands on either side of her, and felt her reach for him, felt her small hands touch his sides, then slide together across his ribs and flatten against his belly, felt her fingers explore. Smiling, he held his breath, letting her discover his flat round nipples, unexpectedly pebbled; the gentle indentation of his navel; the silky places just above his groin. When she touched him there, he sucked in air and lowered his mouth to one tender, pink-tipped breast.

And now it was she who gasped, drawing in one shuddering breath, lifting her breast into his mouth. He felt her fingers curl against his belly as she held the breath, shivering with pleasure at the gentle laving strokes of his tongue. First one, and then the other . . . he hardened his lips, rolling the nipple between them with steadily increasing pressure. Her respirations resumed in sharp, shallow sips. Her hands left his body and moved protectively to her own, as if the sensation were *almost* too much to bear; and when he pulled her nipple deep into his mouth she drew up her knee in a sudden reflexive movement and pressed her hand low on her abdomen, as if she felt the sweet, fierce tugging *there*.

She was writhing and twisting, now, under the taut arch of his body, lifting against the exquisite torment of his mouth, deepening the concavity of her belly. When she moaned softly and spread her fingers wide over the pink-streaked skin below her navel, Culley caught her wrists and took her hands away, and moving lower, pressed his mouth there instead.

Her muscles jumped and fluttered beneath his tongue; her hands gripped his shoulders—hard; and under his stroking hands he felt her thighs tremble. So he soothed and gentled her, petted and teased her, until finally it was she who demanded, pleaded, and guided him with fingers woven through his hair. . . .

When her breath had become sobs and he knew she was hovering on the edge, he slid up over her, letting her know the full weight of his body. She half rose to meet him, seeking his mouth hungrily, receiving him into the cradle of her body with a glad, wordless cry. He had to remind himself, then, to resist the urge to bury himself in her with one joyous thrust, knowing her body was lately unaccustomed to such intrusions, and that he'd surely hurt her if he did. Knowing, too, that even if he did, she probably wouldn't mind.

So once again he gentled her, easing her back from the edge, stroking her forehead and whispering love words against her hot damp skin. And then he closed his eyes, and with restraint quivering through all his muscles, slowly, slowly filled her. The sensation was exquisite, the demands on his self-control excruciating . . . that first, unavoidable break-ing, and her sharp, unconscious gasp . . . and then the relaxing, the shuddering ripples of pleasure, and her little chuckles of relief and joy.

He would have stopped then, and waited for her body to adjust to his alien presence, but she gave a low cry of pure, feminine need and surged against him, wrapping her legs around him, bringing him so deeply into her he knew he didn't have to control himself any longer. With a cry of his own, Culley let go, releasing them both to soar where they would, through a boundless, timeless, trackless place called ecstasy. . . .

Eleven

"No one's ever made me feel like that before," Elizabeth whispered, when the shuddering had stopped and she could speak again.

Culley didn't answer her, but just went on stroking and stroking her forehead. She could feel his heart beating hard and fast against her chest. He'd already tried to shift his weight off her, but she'd held on to him with a cry of protest, afraid to break that intimate contact, afraid to lose that sense of *oneness*, terrified that she might never get it back again.

"I feel . . ." She stopped, closed her eyes, and tilting her chin up, touched a soft, wondering kiss to his damp throat. "I feel beautiful . . . and special . . . and cherished."

"You are . . ." his husky voice vibrated against her lips, ". . . all of the above." She felt him touch his lips to her hair, then gently prod her with his chin. "You know that, don't you?"

There was something about her silence . . . Culley became absolutely still, all his senses alert to everything she wasn't saying.

"Elizabeth?" She closed her eyes and tried to turn away from his intense scrutiny, but he held her, framing her face with his hands. "Dear God," he said harshly, "don't you *know?* Elizabeth, you must know how beautiful you are . . . and how *very* special. And at the very least, you deserve to be cherished. *Don't you know that?*"

A little spasm of pain compressed her lips and dislodged two teardrops that had been there all along, trembling beneath her lashes. She tried to wipe them away with her hands, but he wouldn't let her, taking them himself with his thumbs. And then he released his breath in a long sigh and rolled onto his back, wrapping his arms around her, taking her with him.

There was something wrong here, he thought, something he couldn't quite figure out; and Culley didn't like things he couldn't figure out. There was something going on inside Elizabeth he didn't understand, and he'd had enough of not understanding.

"Elizabeth," he said cautiously when he had her settled to his satisfaction, cradled on his chest with her head tucked under his chin, "a little while ago you asked me a question . . ." His fingers stroked the moisture from her cheek, stroked the hair back from her temples, stroked feathery shivers into her ears. ". . . And I answered it honestly, didn't I?"

She stirred and whispered, "Yes."

"Well, now it's my turn. I'm going to ask you something, and I want you to be as honest."

Elizabeth nodded. Culley's voice and touch were soothing, lulling and gentling her so that instead of alarm or dread she felt only a vague, poignant ache.

"Elizabeth, I want you to tell me what just happened between us."

The question surprised and confused her. She sniffed and said, "I don't know what you mean."

His voice was soft ·but inexorable. "What did we just do?"

Elizabeth closed her eyes, feeling, just feeling. . . . Warm, moist bodies, still tender in places, lying comfortably entwined in such sweet intimacy . . . She whispered, "We . . . made love."

"Yes," he said, with tenderness and a hint of wonder, "We made *love*." And after a moment, with a little rasp in his voice he asked, "How do you feel about that?"

She couldn't answer. Why was it so hard to say the words, she wondered? And how could he not hear them, when they were pealing like church bells inside her?

Culley encouraged her gently. "You said it made you feel . . . beautiful, special, cherished."

She nodded. "Yes."

"But it doesn't make you happy."

She didn't deny it. Culley released his breath and pressed his lips together in silent frustration. And he held her, just held her, one hand covering the side of her face, his fingers burrowing into the warm, damp hair behind her ear, while he tried to put together the pieces of the puzzle.

He knew she was scared. She'd told him so, just a little while ago, and he'd seen it in her himself, more than once. He'd assumed she was afraid of him, for a variety of possible reasons; but he didn't think so now, not after the way she'd responded to him, the way she'd opened to him, even in those first moments of intimacy, with trust and joy.

No, he'd swear she wasn't afraid of him. He arrived at that conclusion by admittedly unscientific means—call it intuition, or gut instinct—but he had a pretty good idea that what Elizabeth was afraid of was her own feelings.

Who's done this to you, Elizabeth? What's happened to make you afraid of love?

And suddenly Culley was scared too. It was a feeling he'd only known once before in his life, when he'd first faced the reality that he might lose Shannon. And now as then, it was mixed with a lot of anger and frustration, because in spite of all his genius, this was something he didn't know how to fix. He couldn't solve this problem. He wasn't a doctor or a miracle worker, and he wasn't a shrink either. He was only a man; and all he knew was that after five lonely years he'd finally found someone to love, and something was keeping her from loving him back.

"Elizabeth," Culley said slowly, feeling as if his life depended on her answer, "how do you feel about me?"

She raised herself on one elbow and frowned confusedly down at him. "How do I feel about you?"

She lifted her hand to wipe moisture from her cheek, turning her face away, evading, stalling . . .

Suddenly Culley couldn't stand it any more. He caught her hand and bore her over on her back, pinning her wrist against the sheets. "Tell me," he said harshly. "It's a fair question—I've already made it pretty clear how I feel about you." Her eyes were like those of a wounded animal. Steeling himself, Culley went ruthlessly on, ignoring her pain because his own was so compelling. "Elizabeth, what just happened between us does not fall into the category of fun and games—not for me, anyway. I want . . . I *need* to know how you feel about me."

"It isn't fun and games for me either," Elizabeth mumbled. She thought, I should have known . . . She should have known he wouldn't let her get away with keeping it locked in her own heart. She, one of the few people in the world who knew what Dr. G. Cullen Ward really was . . . she should have known that he would need to hear the words.

She felt trapped . . . cornered. Trapped by his strong arms and body, by the naked longing in his eyes, by the raw emotion in his voice.

"Elizabeth, do you love me?"

She was a cauldron of emotions, trying desperately to keep the lid on. On a stifled sob she said, "I don't know."

"You don't know? How can you not know?" It was a stupid question, wrung from him by pure frustration. He didn't expect her to answer it, but as he closed his eyes and relaxed in defeat, he felt her seethe beneath him. Words came from her like an eruption.

"Because I don't think I know what love is, that's how!" A great sob tore through her, and he felt her body tense and writhe, almost as if it were something physical, ripping her apart. "Because I loved someone once. I really thought I did. And then . . . I hated him. I *hated* him. I hated him so much I wanted him *dead!*" Her voice was rough, fragmented by those terrible sobs. "Do you know what it's like to hate someone . . . so much . . . you *truly* wish him dead? *Do you?*"

"Oh God," Culley said. "Elizabeth—"

"You thought I was the poor little grieving widow?" Her laugh was harsh and bitter. "Do you want to know how I felt when they told me he was dead? I was relieved. I was so relieved I started to cry, and everyone was so kind to me, so concerned about me. And all the time, all I could think about was that he wasn't ever coming back, I was free, I didn't have to be afraid anymore . . ."

"Elizabeth . . ." Culley let go of her hands, intending to gather her into his arms. Instead, she pushed him away and rolled out of his grasp. He reached for her but she was already out of bed, struggling into his kimono, her hands so jerky she couldn't manage the tie at all.

"So *you* tell me, Culley—how am I supposed to know anything about loving? I've got such a *great* track record!" She hurled that back at him with tears streaming down her face, and then ran out of the room.

Cully said, "Elizabeth—ah . . . *damn!*" He pounded once on the mattress with his fist and then flopped back with his arm across his eyes.

Guilt. That was the thing that had been holding her back all this time—not grief, but guilt. She wasn't grieving for her husband because she'd loved him so much; she was tormenting herself because she hadn't loved him enough.

That knowledge gave Culley no comfort. He knew that grief is like a wound; in most cases, given enough time, a wound heals. But he had an idea that guilt was more like a splinter; left alone it was just going to get worse.

He found her in the living room. She was sitting on the couch with her feet tucked under her, bathed in the soft light from the Christmas tree. She had the green velvet cloak spread across her lap and was stroking it, almost as if it were a living thing. She looked up when she saw Culley in the doorway, but didn't say anything. He folded his arms across his chest and leaned against the doorframe. After a moment she cleared her throat and said, "Merry Christmas."

Culley said, "What?"

She jerked her head toward the fireplace. "The clock struck midnight a little while ago. It's Christmas morning."

"Oh," Culley said. "In that case, Merry Christmas." He unfolded himself and moved into the room. "Shall I . . . light a fire?"

She shrugged. "I'm not cold, but go ahead if you want to."

He did. He'd stopped long enough to put on his pants, but nothing else. When the fire was going he went into the library and got the brandy glasses, poured a good dollop of his Christmas present into each, and handed one to Elizabeth. She shaded her swollen eyes with her hand as she took it, as if he were a light too bright to look at. Culley stood with his back to the fire, swirled the brandy a couple of times and took a swallow. He waited a few minutes, then said, "You didn't kill him, you know."

Her laugh had sharp edges. "I know that. I'm not a child."

"You couldn't have prevented it, either." She sipped brandy and didn't say anything. "Elizabeth, you didn't make him the way he was. What was it—drugs? Alcohol?"

She nodded. "Both."

"He had the problem before you met him, didn't he?" She nodded again. "So how could you be the cause of it?"

She mumbled something Culley couldn't understand. When he said, "What?" she cleared her throat and said painfully, "I made it worse."

"Elizabeth . . ."

"It's true. Kevin was . . . he just couldn't handle stress. Taking on the responsibility of a wife, and then having Wendy—that was my fault, an accident —I should have been—"

"Hold it," Culley interrupted harshly. "Those are the normal stresses of life. If he couldn't handle that, he had a serious problem, and you were not—I repeat, *not*—the cause of it." He put his brandy glass down and went to sit beside her on the couch. "Elizabeth, you've got to let go of the guilt. If you don't, you're not going to be able to put this behind you and get on with your life. Right now it's affecting your self-esteem, your relationships—"

"Isn't this a little out of your line . . . *Doctor* Ward?" she said angrily, tossing back a swallow of brandy. "You're a nuclear physicist, remember? Not a shrink!"

"Dammit, Elizabeth," Culley yelled back at her, "you don't have to be a psychiatrist to see what this is doing to you. Your self-esteem is the pits, you let your in-laws walk all over you, you panic every time Wendy's out of your sight for more than two minutes —why? Did you ever stop to think about that? Why are you always so certain something terrible is going to happen to her? Is it because you think, deep down inside, that you don't deserve something as beautiful and good as she is—"

She slapped him. Culley wrapped his arms around her and hauled her rigid, trembling body hard against him. The brandy snifter tumbled to the carpet and rolled under the coffee table, leaving a dribbling trail of brandy.

Elizabeth's struggle was brief. With a wounded cry she collapsed onto his broad chest, letting his arms come between her and the world, letting his warm hand close out every sound but that of his voice, and his rapidly beating heart. . . .

"Elizabeth, you do deserve good and beautiful things," he said as he rocked her, his voice husky and broken. "You deserve to love, and be loved. You have to believe that."

"I believe—" She cleared her throat and finally said it: "—I do love you." She drew in a shuddering breath and said it again, whispering this time. "I love you. . . ."

Culley didn't answer her, but she felt the ripples of his unspoken feelings pass through his body, like small seismic shockwaves. She felt his lips touch her hair like a tender blessing. And after a while, for the second time that night, outdoing even Rhett Butler, he carried her up the stairs to his bed.

Elizabeth said "I love you" several more times that night, and each time she said it, it got easier. She said it with breathless joy as Culley tumbled her into the wreckage they had earlier made of his bed, then followed her, weighing her down with kisses. She gasped it, half-delirious with desire, as she felt his heat and strength fill her. She whispered it with awe and wonder, holding his face between her hands and gazing deep into his defenseless eyes.

But later, when she lay spent and somnolent on his chest, she stirred and murmured, "I don't believe it."

"What don't you believe?"

"I just can't believe you love me."

Culley's arms tightened around her. "Believe it."

"But . . . I'm not—I haven't—"

"See what I mean about your self-esteem?" He rolled her over and raised himself on one elbow above her. "Elizabeth, how could I not love you?" His eyes weren't defenseless now; they seemed to glow with a light that grew brighter the longer he looked at her, until finally she couldn't bear to look into them anymore.

She closed her eyes and said through the ache in her throat, "It just seems like a miracle to me, that's all."

Culley chuckled and touched a kiss to her throat. "I don't see how you can be surprised. It wasn't exactly sudden. In fact, I think it's been coming on for quite a while. Didn't you have a clue when I filled in the fishpond?"

"No, not then," Elizabeth murmured, giggling because Culley was nuzzling the warm place in the hollow of her neck. "Well . . . maybe a clue—but then you started avoiding me."

"Hmm. When I gave you the locket, surely . . ."

"No," said Elizabeth, smiling. "Not then. But I think I knew . . . I knew when you gave me Princess Kerissa's cloak."

He chuckled. "Well, I suppose that was—" And then she felt his body tense. He caught a handful of her hair and stared down into her face. "Princess Kerissa's—how did you—" The struggle to regain control of his own features was comical to behold. "Well." He coughed. "That is . . . oh, I see, you mean because Wendy thought it looked like . . ."

But Elizabeth was shaking her head. She smiled and said gently, "No."

Culley's body deflated. He closed his eyes and said, "Oh Lord. How long have you known?"

She reached up and took his face between her hands. "That you are the elusive G. C. Wardlaw, creator of Solar and Kerissa, author of *The Antarian Trilogy*, and . . ." she kissed him tenderly, ". . . the biggest romantic since King Arthur?"

"Yeah, that."

"Since the first week I was in this house. I didn't mean to, I swear. Wendy got into your office through the kitty door and was having such a wonderful time, she wouldn't come out. I had to take the door off the hinges."

Culley groaned. "It figures. All this time I've been trying to figure out how in the world to tell you." He scowled. "It's not an easy thing to own up to, you know."

Elizabeth saw, to her great delight, that he was blushing. That was when she said it for the last time that night: "Dr. Ward, or Wardlaw, or whoever you are . . . *I love you.*"

They slept late on Christmas morning, then showered together, exploring each other's bodies as if neither of them had ever seen one before. They ate Christmas cookies and drank fresh orange juice for breakfast, then set about making stuffing for the Christmas goose while the kittens frolicked and tumbled and got in the way.

Culley said he'd never eaten a goose before; Elizabeth told him she'd never cooked one before, so they were even.

And they talked. Culley told Elizabeth about how he'd come to write the first Solar adventures, as an escape from the loneliness and pain after Shannon's death, and how amazed he'd been at their phenomenal success. Elizabeth told Culley how she'd come to Los Angeles to escape the pain of her father's slow deterioration, and what it had felt like to be alone and friendless in a strange city, vulnerable to the first man who paid any attention to her.

"Kevin really was crazy about me," she said pensively. "It was great for my ego. He was tall, handsome, blond, clean-cut, a beautiful boy. And he thought I was the greatest thing to come along since sliced bread."

It was evening. They'd eaten dinner and done the dishes and then walked in the grounds until dusk and cold had driven them indoors. Now they were curled up on the couch in front of the fireplace, sipping Culley's Christmas brandy.

"He saw something in you that he didn't have," Culley said. "It's called inner strength. I saw it in you, too, that first night when you came to my door. You reminded me of a lioness."

Elizabeth smiled at him and said, "Hmm." Her eyes strayed to the clock on the mantel.

Catching the look, Culley asked casually, "When's the squirt due back?"

A little furrow appeared between Elizabeth's eyes. "They said they'd bring her back this evening. I didn't set an exact time. I guess I should have. It's after six, and Wendy's bedtime is about seven."

"If you're concerned, why don't you call?"

Elizabeth threw him a grateful look and went out to the kitchen to make the call. In a few minutes she was back, looking happier.

"Nobody's answering, so I guess they must be on the way. It's only about a half hour's drive, so they could be here any minute."

Culley hugged her and said, "Good. I've missed the little imp. I have to tell you—I love her, too, you know."

She was too misty to answer, so she kissed him instead.

Half an hour later she was pacing back and forth in front of the fireplace, looking at the clock every two minutes and exclaiming irritably, "Where in the world can they be?"

"They probably just stopped somewhere to get something to eat," Culley told her soothingly. "People do eat on Christmas Day too, you know. Maybe they stopped at McDonald's."

"Wendy loves McDonald's . . ." But the worry lines between Elizabeth's eyes didn't go away.

But by eight o'clock, Culley was beginning to worry, too. He'd run out of reassurances for Elizabeth, and had been reduced to murmuring inane things like, "Don't worry, I'm sure there's a logical explanation." But for the life of him, he couldn't think of one.

Elizabeth was a basket case. She kept bouncing back and forth between anger and despair. One minute she'd be raging at herself—"I should never have let her go!"—or the Resnicks—"How could they do this to me!"—or Fate—"Why does something always happen to spoil everything!" And the next minute she'd be curled up in an inconsolable ball, sobbing, "Oh God, please let her be all right . . ."

And there wasn't anything Culley could do to make it better.

Fighting his own fears, he began calling the Resnicks' house every fifteen minutes. He called the highway patrol and asked if there'd been any accidents reported in the general area. He called hospitals. He couldn't bring himself to call the morgue.

"If anything bad had happened, we'd know about it," he told Elizabeth. "We'd have been notified."

She looked at him. The calm logic of her reply chilled him. "How would they know? Wendy doesn't wear a tag saying, 'In case of emergency, notify . . .' And I doubt very much that the Resnicks do either." She lapsed back into silence . . . pale and numb.

Culley's own rage and dread were mounting. He felt so *helpless*. He wanted to do something—smash something, yell, cry. But there wasn't anything he could do except sit and tell himself it was going to be all right, and watch the excruciating suffering of the woman he loved.

It was one of the longest and worst evenings of his life. In some ways it brought back memories of the long vigils at Shannon's bedside in the last days of her life. But there had been an inevitability about that, and at the end, a quiet acceptance. This was different, and so much worse.

He kept seeing Wendy's sparkling eyes, her pixie grin, feeling her chubby arms wrapped octopuslike around his legs, hearing her delighted crow, "Daddy!"

He thought, Why do I want to put myself through this? A person has to be *crazy* to become a parent!

At five minutes before ten, they saw car lights come around the drive and stop in front of the house. Elizabeth stood up slowly. Culley went to the window and looked out. When he saw that it wasn't an official vehicle of any kind, he experienced a strange, cold, hollow feeling. Relief, he assumed. Relief and pure unadulterated rage.

He turned calmly and said to Elizabeth, "Do the Resnicks drive a Cadillac?"

She nodded, and carefully wiped her face with her hands. Culley wordlessly put out his hand and pulled her against his side, and they walked together into the hallway. Just before he opened the front door, he gave her a little squeeze and whispered gruffly, "You okay?" She nodded.

They watched Carl Resnick get out of the car and go around to open the back door on the passenger side. He bent down, then straightened with Wendy in his arms—a sound asleep Wendy, wearing a new blue jacket with a fur collar. She was clutching her tattered blanket, and what looked like a new Winnie-the-Pooh. Margaret Resnick opened her door and got out, struggling to control two large helium balloons with Mickey Mouse ears.

Culley felt as if the top of his head were about to blow off.

As Carl came up the steps he grinned and said in a loud whisper, "Hi, sorry we're a little later than we planned. As you can see, Wendy's had quite a day. She's pretty well worn out. If you want, I can just take her—"

"Culley—" Elizabeth put a hand on his arm. "Would you mind taking her upstairs for me? I'd like to talk to Carl and Margaret for a minute." Her voice was calm. Too calm.

Carl transferred the sleeping child to Culley's arms. Culley looked over the tousled blond head at Elizabeth and murmured, "Are you going to be all right?"

She smiled at him, and stood on tiptoe to kiss him. "I'm going to be . . . just *fine*," she whispered, laying her hand briefly on her daughter's head. "I'll be in in just a minute, okay?"

Culley hesitated, then nodded and went into the house, leaving Elizabeth to face her dragons alone.

When the door had closed behind Culley, there was an awkward little silence, and then Margaret stepped forward with the balloons. "Here, Elizabeth, if you want to take these, I'll just get Wendy's things—"

"You didn't tell me you were planning to go to Disneyland," Elizabeth said, cutting her short.

"Well, it was kind of a spur of the moment thing," Carl drawled, shifting a little. "We probably should have called, but doggone it, we were just having a real good time, and since I hadn't actually said what time we'd be back, I didn't think you'd be too worried. Were you worried? Liz, honey, you know we wouldn't—"

"I was worried," Elizabeth interrupted in a firm, clear voice. "Very worried. And you should have called. Carl, I must insist that in the future you not take Wendy out of the immediate area without first notifying me and getting my permission. Is that clear?"

Carl looked taken aback. "Well, sure, honey, if that's what you want. Sure, I understand."

Margaret hesitated, then thrust the balloon strings into Elizabeth's hands and started down the steps. "I'll just get Wendy's things out of the trunk," she said, sounding out of breath.

"Not now," Elizabeth said firmly. "It's late. Wendy and I'll be over in a few days; I'll get them then. I want to discuss a plan for regularly scheduled visits with you, if that's convenient." She made it a polite statement, not a question.

The good-byes took only a moment; Elizabeth was safely back inside the house before reaction set in.

"I did it," she said to Culley, who was just coming back down the stairs.

"What did you do, love?" he asked her with shining eyes.

She told him, through chattering teeth, and then gave a little shriek of surprise when he shouted, "Bravo!" and picked her up, whirled her around in his arms and hugged her until her ribs squeaked.

The telephone rang at three o'clock in the morning. Culley picked up the receiver on the nightstand and mumbled, "H'lo?"

"Oh darling—did I wake you?" a distant voice said. "I'm so sorry. I get the time differences mixed up. I just called to wish you a Merry Christmas. Of course, it's already past Christmas here—"

"It's past Christmas here, too, Mother. It's three in the morning."

"It is? Oh dear. Oh well. Did you have a nice Christmas? How are Elizabeth and Wendy?"

"They're fine, Mother. Just fine." He smiled at Elizabeth, whose head was just rising above his shoulder like a red-gold sun.

"Wish them both a very Merry Christmas for me, will you?"

"Want to wish her one yourself?" Ignoring Elizabeth's frantic gestures and efforts to shush him, Culley chuckled and said, "She's right here. . . . Sweetheart, it's Mom. She says 'Merry Christmas.' "

Elizabeth put her hand over her eyes and squeaked, "Merry Christmas, Mrs. Ward."

There was a long silence on the other end of the line. And then, to Culley's astonishment, a shout of pure delight. "Oh! Oh, thank goodness! It's about time. Does this mean I can come home now? Do you have any idea how long I've been waiting for you two to come to your senses? I've been so homesick—I'm so tired of tropical islands I could *die!*"

When Culley finally cradled the phone a few minutes later he was looking bemused. "Elizabeth," he said slowly, "I think we've been set up."

"Hmm?"

"I think my mother may have planned this whole thing. Do you mind being the victim of a matchmaker?"

"Do I act like I mind?"

"Hmm . . . I sure don't. Not if you keep doing that . . ."

"What doin', Mommy?"

"Oh God," Culley and Elizabeth groaned in unison, raising their heads to gaze in dismay at the sunny yellow head that was hovering at the foot of the bed.

"You're definitely going to have to find a solution for that problem," Culley muttered darkly.

"Me! You're the genius."

"Hmm. We'll work on it together. But we'd better come up with something. *Quickly* . . ."

"Very quickly," Elizabeth agreed. "I sure don't want Wendy to be an only child."

And Culley fervently replied, "Not a chance."

Wendy woke and sat up in bed, shivering. She wasn't cold and she wasn't frightened . . . not really. She had her blankie and she knew Mommy and Daddy were right nearby, in the big bed in Daddy's room. She just wanted someone to hold her and make her feel warm and safe and cozy.

She thought about getting out of bed and going down the hall and getting in bed with Mommy and Daddy. Her door was locked, but there was that brand new kitty door that Daddy had made just this morning. She was getting almost too big for the kitty doors now, but maybe if she squeezed . . .

But if she got out of her bed, Mommy would be angry with her, and maybe Daddy would be too. She didn't want Daddy to be angry with her. Even the thought made her feel like crying.

Wendy thought about crying. Maybe, if she cried very loudly, someone would come to see what was the matter.

And then she heard a sound. A warm, furry sound. It was coming from a shadow near the foot of her bed. When she wiggled her toes, the shadow moved and said, "Mew?"

Wendy gave a little gasp of surprise and whispered, "Kitties!"

Tiny velvet footsteps padded across her legs and into her lap; a tiny velvet nose bumped her tummy. Chuckling happily, Wendy lay back down and snuggled into her pillow. The kitten padded across her chest, crawled under the covers, curled up on her tummy and began to purr. The purring made Wendy feel warm and safe and cozy. In a very few minutes she was sound asleep.

THE EDITOR'S CORNER

Bantam Books has a *very* special treat for you next month—Nora Roberts's most ambitious, most sizzling novel yet . . .

SWEET REVENGE

Heroine Adrianne, the daughter of a fabled Hollywood beauty and an equally fabled Arab playboy, leads a remarkable double life. The paparazzi and the gossip columnists know her as a modern princess, a frivolous socialite flitting from exclusive watering spot to glittering charity ball. No one knows her as The Shadow, the most extraordinary jewel thief of the decade. She hones her skills at larceny as she parties with the superrich, stealing their trinkets and baubles just for practice . . . for she has a secret plan for the ultimate heist—a spectacular plan to even a bitter score. Her secret is her own until Philip Chamberlain enters her life. Once a renowned thief himself, he's now one of Interpol's smartest, toughest cops . . . and he's falling wildly in love with Adrianne!

SWEET REVENGE will be on sale during the beginning of December when your LOVESWEPTs come into the stores. Be sure to ask your bookseller right now to reserve a copy especially for you.

Now to the delectable LOVESWEPTs you can count on to add to your holiday fun . . . and excitement.

Our first love story next month carries a wonderful round number—LOVESWEPT #300! **LONG TIME COMING**, by Sandra Brown, is as thrilling and original as any romance Sandra has ever written. Law Kincaid, the heart-stoppingly handsome astronaut hero, is in a towering rage when he comes storming up Marnie Hibbs's front walk. He thinks she has been sending him blackmail letters claiming he has a teenage son. As aghast as she is, and still wildly attracted to Law, whom she met seventeen years before when she was just a teen, Marnie tries to put him off and hold her secret close. But the golden and glorious man is determined to wrest the truth from her at any cost! A beautiful love story!

(continued)

Welcome back Peggy Webb, author of LOVESWEPT #301, **HALLIE'S DESTINY,** a marvelous love story featuring a gorgeous "gypsy" whom you met in previous books, Hallie Donovan. A rodeo queen with a heart as big as Texas, Hallie was the woman Josh Butler wanted—he knew it the second he set eyes on her! Josh was well aware of the havoc a bewitching woman like Hallie could wreak in a man's life, but he couldn't resist her. When Josh raked her with his sexy golden eyes and took her captive on a carpet of flowers, Hallie felt a miraculous joy . . . and a great fear, for Josh couldn't—wouldn't—share his life and its problems with her. He sets limits on their love that drive Hallie away . . . until neither can endure without the other. A thrilling romance!

New author Gail Douglas scores another winner with **FLIRTING WITH DANGER,** LOVESWEPT #302. Cassie Walters is a spunky and gorgeous lady who falls under the spell of Bret Parker, a self-made man who is as rich as he is sexy . . . and utterly relentless when it comes to pursuing Cassie. Bret's not quite the womanizer the press made him out to be, as Cassie quickly learns. (I think you'll relish as much as I did the scene in which Michael and Cassie see each other for the first time. Never has an author done more for baby powder and diapers than Gail does in that encounter!) Cassie is terrified of putting down roots . . . and Bret is quite a family man. He has to prove to the woman with whom he's fallen crazily in love that she is brave enough to share his life. A real charmer of a love story crackling with excitement!

In **MANHUNT,** LOVESWEPT #303, Janet Evanovich has created two delightfully adorable and lusty protagonists in a setting that is fascinating. Alexandra Scott—fed up with her yuppie life-style and yearning for a husband and family— has chucked it all and moved to the Alaskan wilderness. She hasn't chosen her new home in a casual way; she's done it using statistics—in Alaska men outnumber women four to one. And right off the bat she meets a man who's one in a million, a dizzyingly attractive avowed bachelor, Michael Casey. But Alex can't be rational about Michael; she loses her head, right along with her heart to him. And to capture him she has to be shameless in her seduction. . . . A true delight!

Get ready to be transported into the heart of a small Southern town and have your funny bone tickled while your

(continued)

heart is warmed when you read **RUMOR HAS IT**, LOVE-SWEPT #304, by Tami Hoag. The outrageous gossip that spreads about Nick Leone when he comes to town to open a restaurant has Katie Quaid as curious as every other woman in the vicinity. She's known as an ice princess, but the moment she and Nick get together she's melting for him. You may shed a tear for Katie—she's had unbearable tragedy in her young life—and you'll certainly gasp with her when Nick presents her with a shocking surprise. A wonderfully fresh and emotionally moving love story!

That marvelous Nick Capoletti you met in Joan Elliott Pickart's last two romances gets his own true love in **SERENITY COVE**, LOVESWEPT #305. When Pippa Pauling discovered Nick Capoletti asleep on the floor of the cabin he'd rented in her cozy mountain lake resort, she felt light-headed with longing and tempted beyond resistance. From the second they first touched, Nick knew Pippa was hearth and home and everything he wanted in life. But Pippa feared that the magic they wove was fleeting. No one could fall in love so fast and make it real for a lifetime. But leave it to Capoletti! In a thrilling climax that takes Pippa and Nick back to Miracles Casino in Las Vegas and the gang there, Pippa learns she can indeed find forever in Nick's arms. A scorching and touching romance from our own Joan Elliott Pickart!

Also in Bantam's general list next month is a marvelous mainstream book that features love, murder, and shocking secrets—**MIDNIGHT SINS**, by new author Ellin Hall. This is a fast-paced and thrilling book with an unforgettable heroine. Don't miss it.

Have a wonderful holiday season.

Carolyn Nichols

Carolyn Nichols
Editor
LOVESWEPT
Bantam Books
666 Fifth Avenue
New York, NY 10103

THE DELANEY DYNASTY

Men and women whose loves and passions are so glorious it takes many great romance novels by three bestselling authors to tell their tempestuous stories.

THE SHAMROCK TRINITY

- ☐ 21786 RAFE, THE MAVERICK
  by Kay Hooper $2.75
- ☐ 21787 YORK, THE RENEGADE
  by Iris Johansen $2.75
- ☐ 21788 BURKE, THE KINGPIN
  by Fayrene Preston $2.75

THE DELANEYS OF KILLAROO

- ☐ 21872 ADELAIDE, THE ENCHANTRESS
  by Kay Hooper $2.75
- ☐ 21873 MATILDA, THE ADVENTURESS
  by Iris Johansen $2.75
- ☐ 21874 SYDNEY, THE TEMPTRESS
  by Fayrene Preston $2.75

- ☐ 26991 THIS FIERCE SPLENDOR
  by Iris Johansen $3.95

Now Available!

THE DELANEYS: *The Untamed Years*

- ☐ 21897 GOLDEN FLAMES *by Kay Hooper* $3.50
- ☐ 21898 WILD SILVER *by Iris Johansen* $3.50
- ☐ 21999 COPPER FIRE *by Fayrene Preston* $3.50

Buy these books at your local bookstore or use this page to order:

- -

Bantam Books, Dept. SW7, 414 East Golf Road, Des Plaines, IL 60016

Please send me the books I have checked above. I am enclosing $_____ (please add $2.00 to cover postage and handling). Send check or money order—no cash or C.O.D.s please.

Mr/Ms _____

Address _____

City/State _____ Zip _____

SW7—10/88

Please allow four to six weeks for delivery. This offer expires 4/89. Prices and availability subject to change without notice.